# AD LIMINA

a novella of

Catholics

in space

This book is a work of fiction. Any resemblance to persons living or dead, actual events, locales, or organizations is either coincidental or satirical.

Published by March 7 Media
March7Media.com

ISBN-13: 978-0615781501 (March 7 Media)

ISBN-10: 0615781500

Cover art by Lucas Turnbloom

"Every five years … a diocesan bishop is to go to Rome to venerate the tombs of the Blessed Apostles Peter and Paul and to present himself to the Roman Pontiff."

**Code of Canon Law for the
Latin Rite Catholic Church
(Promulgated 1983)**

"In cases of travel hardship, the bishop of a diocese outside the orbit of Earth's moon may delay, with permission of the Holy See, otherwise required visits to the tombs of the Blessed Apostles…"

**Code of Canon Law for the
Latin Rite Catholic Church
(Promulgated 2098)**

# PROLOGUE

"Humanity fears the fire. It is in our nature to fear the fire.

"But the vanguard does not fear the fire.

"The vanguard wields it.

"There can be no morality, no peace, nothing of beauty in humanity unless the vanguard wields the purifying fire.

"What has humanity become but a craven animal lost to its passions?

"But if they will become less than men, we will become more than men in order to save them, in order to make of humanity the glorious thing it can be.

"We will become men of fire and power in order to lead them back, so that they can at least be men of flesh and bone.

"Soon the Fuhrer will restore all men.

"There are many who could be men who are now craven animals, if only the vanguard would return them to their senses and furnish them with a purpose.

"We are the few who will know true glory, and there will never be more than a few.

"But when we have come to power, all men will be raised up.

"The moment is coming. It is near.

"The vanguard will fall on them in all their immorality and laziness.

"The Fuhrer will descend onto the Earth like a purifying fire."

**Vice Fuhrer Eugenio Sacco,**
**Introducing Fuhrer Joseph Hadamar**
**Party Congress Seven, New Nuremberg**

# (1.)

The Bishop of Mars had to take one of the giant, six-wheeled delivery wagons from Coolidge-town to the unregistered port of Sakharov. There a scramjet was to take him up to the second-class passenger ship Frank Sinatra for the trip to Earth.

Just to see what would happen, the bishop had tried to book passage on one of the big, comfortable UNAC liners. "You never know until you try," he thought. There was always the possibility of some kind of administrative lapse.

He probably shouldn't have been so naïve. His attempt to book UNAC passage made news all over Mars, and even on Earth. The press assumed he was attempting to make some political statement by applying, and his assertion that the whole thing had been a sincere effort simply to arrange travel had been dismissed out of hand.

As an official of the Catholic Church he was naturally on the no-fly list. Catholic bishops do not apply for passage on a registered ship.

The whole incident had been dumb and depressing. The Mars Area Minister of Security had lectured the bishop publicly for days on interview shows about the seriousness of fleet security measures. Several editorials had appeared reminding the bishop that—even though Catholics themselves were an intolerant sect—they were tolerated by the good people of Mars. The implication was clear: such tolerance could be rescinded should the bishop care to keep making an ass of himself.

He had even received a letter from the UNAC—a letter that was also leaked to the press—in which members of the Human Rights Committee dressed him down for the outrageousness of wanting to avail himself of UNAC transport even while holding views that discriminated against group marriages, genetically modified people, etc.

The worst part was that he had, for a brief moment, become something of a hero to the Fascists, who took the episode to be political theater, of which they heartily approved.

It was a bit frightening to spend those several days in the hot glare of public scrutiny. He did not recognize himself in the things people said and wrote about him, whether hostile or supportive.

It was as if the great communications devices, the screens and the networks and the satellites, all had built within them a pressing need that something—anything—be said. There was an implicit demand in all the technology of mass communication, a demand that humanity never stop talking, analyzing, reaching conclusions, forming opinions. And humanity obliged, pouring out words to serve the gaping need built into the system.

Fortunately, the underlying transgression had not really been that great, and so the story faded.

Like other Catholic officials around the solar system, the bishop arranged unregistered transport and quietly booked a cabin on the delivery wagon that would take him to Sakharov, where he could board the Frank Sinatra.

Such inconveniences were part of his job. While getting to the main port in Coolidge would have meant riding a pair of escalators and walking a few blocks south of the Coolidge Commons, to take unregulated transport he had to make his way far outside the city and into a kind of wilderness.

Sakharov did not strike terror in the heart—as some of the Jovian colonies did—but it had a slightly seedy reputation. And other than the reputation, all the bishop really knew of the place was that they mined deuterium, they had a good water supply, and tourists who were making ground tours of the planet often visited to take pressure-suit hikes through the nearby canyons.

Sakharov had no parish, but it had an elderly Dominican missionary originally from South Africa. Technically, the place was not part of the Diocese of Mars, but was one of several odd spots on the planet that remained under missionary jurisdiction, and the bishop had never had occasion to visit.

The main problem with Sakharov was that it was hard to get to. Nothing that flew and wanted to keep its UNAC License could go there because the city founders were libertarians, and the only available ground transport was the big, off-road delivery wagons, which mainly transported supplies and— mostly as an afterthought—made room for passengers.

Even to get on the delivery wagon, the bishop had to take the train out to Filmoreville, which was called a town but was really not much more than a few tunnels and a Denny's. From there he had to catch a surface cab out of UNAC territory to a big duty-free warehouse filled with supplies and lifters and delivery wagons. When loaded, the wagons hauled the supplies to outposts all over the surrounding area.

He'd met up with his wagon as it was being loaded and found out that it would be making three stops before Sakharov, a trip that would take a night and a day. His cabin was a cramped little space with a bed and a bathroom, and about enough floor space to walk between the bed and the wall.

He genuinely liked it. Something about its smallness made him delight in it: his own little secret compartment on the side of a four-story-tall truck. And it had a window to watch Mars roll by. Alone here, he could say his prayers and daydream and sleep without worries.

Even with its articulated suspension and its six giant wheels, however, the delivery wagon was a bouncy ride as it made its way across the volcano-scarred Tharsis Plateau. It made the bishop a little seasick, and he was anxious to get out and walk on solid ground at the first stop. The screen said, "Marti. Thirty minute stop. Passengers may disembark. Transport will not wait for late returnees. Next transport, two sols."

He had never been to Marti, and he had no priest here. The town's entry port was—like all ports—a warehouse with a big door. The wagon drove in, and then the port operator sealed the door behind them before pressuring the warehouse back up with breathable atmosphere.

Once the atmosphere in the warehouse was at pressure, the delivery wagon opened its hatches and passengers dismounted single file down a narrow ramp. Signs on the concrete walls pointed to the town entrance. The bishop followed these, and stepped into the first lock with a group of ten or so tired-looking fellow travelers. The air locks cycled through quickly, and they were through the third in less than a minute.

It opened onto a town that the bishop found surprisingly beautiful. Most of it was a rock formation that had been left in its natural state. It was a few hundred meters long and a couple hundred wide. It appeared to have been an open cave, kind of a big indent in the side of a mountain. Settlers had sealed its open side with concrete and built homes and businesses along the mountain wall. The place looked like it could support a population of two or three hundred.

The founders of the town obviously hadn't had the money for gelglass, so there was no real view. Instead, there were high-res Samsung screens set at intervals along the wall to act as virtual windows. High-res cameras mounted outside the wall fed images in.

The passengers meeting the delivery wagon here were not from Marti. They were from Hayes, a city of thirty thousand some twenty-five kilometers south. Just as Filmoreville served as the nearest unregulated outpost to Coolidge, so Marti served for Hayes. People came out here for transport if they were on the no-fly list—Mormons, Fascists, Catholics, Jehovah's Witnesses, nationalists, neo-moralists, Australians, and so on.

It was late evening, and most of Marti was sleeping. The four new passengers who were checking in all looked tired and a bit disheveled after their trip from Hayes.

That is, except one. The bishop found himself wondering about this figure: a young man, thirty-five years old perhaps, whose clothes were informal but impeccable. He carried nothing but a small, elegant bag. He showed little sign of fatigue. And his manners as he dealt with the check-in process were both precise and unstrained. How had this worldly traveler come to be on the no-fly list?

With a solid twenty minutes before he was to depart, the bishop bought a cup of decaf from the port snack bar and allowed himself a ten-minute stroll along Marti's only street.

# (2.)

Back in his quarters, the bishop took a dose of anti-seasickness nasal spray and read in his bunk. Before long, he tired of the book and curled up to the window. It was dark outside, and the stars were magnificent. The rocking of the wagon was pleasant now that he had taken the spray and soothing enough to send him off to sleep.

He dreamt of diving in the Chasm Sea, the human-made body of water a kilometer beneath Coolidge. He loved this little sea that had been built after the people of Coolidge came upon an enormous natural cavern during an exploratory dig. They had filled it with comet-mined water to create a place for breeding fish and for their own recreation. He spent much of his free time exploring it and had spent hours lazily floating over the sea grasses, breathing quietly through his snorkel and marveling at the mysterious beauty that accrues to anything submerged. He cherished any opportunity to swim with the black sea bass, the seals, and the leopard sharks.

A team of technicians kept the water chemically balanced and properly heated. The animals were imports, transported across millions of miles of space as frozen embryos. Even the sky above the half kilometer-wide sea—with its blue shimmering brightness suggesting a nearby sun and a thick atmosphere—was a digital projection from a specially designed Samsung unit.

A fake sea under a fake sky.

But though it was all just an imitation of Earth, the Chasm Sea was one of the wonders of Mars.

He dreamt of Earth, and in his dream it was a thickly forested place. In the forest he could hear bears and catch glimpses of their powerful shoulders as they foraged and grunted all around him.

He dreamt of scramjets and immense Martian dirigibles and then of delivery wagons, great fleets of them, rolling in formation as if to war.

He slept through the next stop, a calcium sulfate mine, and awoke to daylight. The media unit in his little room told him that eight hours remained until Sakharov.

He showered, dressed, and repacked his bags, setting them neatly on the bed. That done, he headed out to see what might be available for breakfast.

There were two common rooms on the wagon. One had a dozen or so media lounges, and the other was a cafeteria with long tables and an ordering counter.

He grasped the railing at the counter to steady himself against the bobbing and rolling of the floor.

He asked for toast and coffee. An older woman in a smock served him and charged him 3.5 Unies. He sat down at one of the cafeteria tables—he was not really interested in the media lounges—made the sign of the cross, and offered a little prayer before starting on the toast.

Across the nearly empty room, his eyes met those of the elegant young man from Marti. The bishop nodded and offered a friendly smile.

The young man nodded in return, stood, collected his own breakfast onto a tray, and made his way toward the bishop.

"You pray before eating," he said, when he reached the bishop.

"I do," the bishop answered. "Is that something you are interested in?"

"Very much," the young man said. "May I join you?"

"Oh, excuse me, I should have ... of course. Please, sit down."

"Thank you." The young man sat. He offered the bishop his hand. "David Elsman."

"Pleased to meet you, David," the bishop said, shaking the offered hand. "Mark Gastelum."

"A pleasure, Mark," David said. He had an easy way about him, friendly, courteous, but not in the least self-conscious.

"Are you headed off-planet?" the bishop asked, not forgetting about David's prayer remark, but not returning to it too quickly, either.

"To Earth," David said, "on the mighty Frank Sinatra, which seems to be the only ship in the solar system willing to have me."

"That hardly seems likely."

"Well, I have been to Ceres," the young man offered by way of explanation.

This genuinely surprised the bishop. The young man did not give off the slightest hint of Fascism.

"I'm not a Fascist," David said, apparently spotting the puzzlement on the bishop's face. "I am an academic. I write about the Fascists, and I managed to get myself invited to visit headquarters, so to speak."

"Without UNAC permission?"

"Can't get permission; Ceres is off limits. But it's not hard to get to. Once you get out to the station colonies, you can get transport anywhere. The problem is that the Fleet has ways of knowing who visits Ceres, so when I got back here to Mars, I was held for questioning. I explained my scholarly interest. They explained to me that I was now under a security travel ban, and that was that. When I get back to Oxford, I'll try to get a hearing to get the ban lifted."

The bishop took all this in without comment.

"And what about you?" the young man asked. "Where to?"

"The Frank Sinatra, as well. I am a Catholic bishop, and that makes me an officer in a 'systematically discriminatory organization.'"

"Shame on you," the young man said slyly. "But that does explain the prayer."

"I suppose it does. You were saying that prayer is an interest of yours?"

"Yes, I started out studying religions. I am a sociologist, and I was always interested in the human capacity to be interested in the supernatural. As a scholar of religion yourself, you can see how that would lead to my current interest in the Fascists."

David watched the bishop, perhaps waiting for some response, but the bishop continued listening silently.

"Of course, they are not religious in the Christian sense," David went on. "But they are religious in the sense that they use symbolism and ceremony to generate powerful shared experiences— experiences that they find transcendent and meaningful."

"I am actually not much of a scholar," the bishop said as he took another bite of toast, "but I can see what you mean."

The young man, openly passionate about his topic, was clearly pleased to have someone with whom to share his thinking. "They are religious without God. That is ... well, without sounding rude, the fundamental difference between them and a Christian such as yourself. Does that come across as insulting?"

"Not at all." The bishop grinned and sipped his tea. "I would say the difference between having God and not having Him is about the most significant difference you could have."

"Just so. But it is remarkable how much religion there is among people who claim no God. The ritual, the group experience, it is all very similar."

"Among the New Progressivist majority, too," the bishop said.

It seemed to take the young man a moment to assess whether or not he was being challenged. "Well, yes, of course," he said at last. "I suppose that is the whole point of my academic career, sussing out just which things we do because they are rational and which things we do because they meet what I suppose we could call our religious need."

The bishop nodded. "Do you think our religious need corresponds to something real?"

"That is not for me to say," the young man said, "it may indeed. What I know I can say is that it does not always correspond to something good. That is to say, religion—say the way the Fascists use it—can be a means of ugliness."

The bishop nodded again.

"I hope this is not coming across wrong," David said.

"Do you know what a catechism is?"

"Yes, I think I do, a kind of text or video that gives the basic teachings of a religion."

"Yes, right," the bishop said. "The earliest surviving Catholic catechism text was written within maybe a hundred years of Christ's death. And it begins with these words, 'There are two ways, the way of life and the way of death, and there is much difference between the two.'"

For a moment, the young man made no reply but stared at the bishop as if waiting for the point.

Seeing that the young man had not gotten the point, the bishop went on. "They were talking about exactly what you are talking about. Why do you think they wrote, 'there is much difference between the two?'"

The young man shrugged, willing to play along, but not getting whatever insight the bishop was trying to share.

The bishop smiled. "They wrote it because it is not obvious. The way of life and the way of death look very much the same. They use the same terminology. They use the same symbols and rituals in many cases. But they are not the same. There is much difference between the two."

"Ah, yes, I see," David said politely but somewhat vacantly. "I suppose that is exactly what I am talking about. The Fascists are deeply religious without having real religion, at least not in the ways we think of religion."

It seemed to the bishop that the young man had not gotten his point at all. "Are you religious?"

"Not in a traditional sense, but I do have a sense that religion is not empty, that it is in some way about something vital."

"God, maybe?"

"Something ineffable. Perhaps God is the word for it. I couldn't say. But I do believe that spiritual experience is real, or anyway some of it is."

"Not a naturalist, then?"

"I don't know. Maybe I am a naturalist who just believes that nature has more to offer than we can get at rationally. Or maybe not ... that is, maybe there is something beyond nature."

"There is," the bishop said with mock authority, pantomiming as if to pound his fist on the table. "The rumors are true."

The young man laughed. "I wish I could be as sure as you."

# (3.)

David Elsman had barely gotten to visit Mars. He had come in on a transport from a station colony, been held for questioning, and then been told to take the first available transport off planet.

Trying to make up for the young man's lost opportunity to sightsee, the bishop spent most of his morning describing life on the red planet.

"Well, no, Coolidge is not much like Hayes," the bishop said. Hayes was the only Martian town David had been able to visit. "First of all, Coolidge is about three times as big—the biggest city on Mars—and it goes much deeper into the planet."

"And the people are still burrowing down deeper?"

"That is what we do on Mars, we build and we burrow."

"How deep does Coolidge warren go?"

"I suppose about a kilometer, maybe more in places," the bishop answered, "and it spreads out over an area of several kilometers. But I should tell you, only Earth people call it a warren. Here on Mars, we just call it a city. We think of a warren as a small town."

"On Earth, Coolidge would be a small town."

"But to us, it is a metropolis," the bishop replied, feigning indignation. "The center of it is an 18-story vertical open space that the Corps of Engineers bored and blasted out of solid rock and then covered with a 250-meter wide gelglass skylight to make the city commons."

"It sounds magnificent."

"I wish you could have seen it," the bishop said.

"So why are you going to Earth?" David asked when there was a lull in the descriptions of Mars.

"Called to Rome," the bishop said with a shrug.

"To live on Earth?"

"Oh, no. Every five years, a Catholic bishop has to make what is called an *Ad Limina Apostolorum*. Basically, we have to check in with the pope."

"How many times have you gone?"

"This will be the first Ad Limina visit ever made by a bishop of Mars. We are still considered mission territory, and before I became bishop, our bishops had all been old men sent to finish their lives far from home. They were missionaries in the old sense, and they knew when they accepted the assignment to Mars it was a one-way ticket."

"They must have been very dedicated."

"Yes, they were. And you have to remember, before these newer rocket motors, the crossing from Mars to Earth was an even longer and harder journey than it is now. If you came out here as an old man, there was no way you were making that crossing again."

"But things have changed now, with the combination of the new motors and a young bishop, it is time for a visit to Rome?"

"Yes. I will probably be the bishop here for thirty or forty years. I suppose that will mean making quite a few crossings to Earth."

"Are you very young for a bishop?"

"I was when I was ordained. I was just a warren parish priest of forty-one when I got the call. I was shocked to suddenly be the prelate of a whole planet—even if it is a planet of barely two million souls with only about two or three percent of them practicing Catholics."

"They don't give you any warning? They just call you up and tell you that you are the new bishop?"

The bishop chuckled at this. "Basically, yes. I thought at the time that Rome would send an older priest from Earth or maybe just assign the abbot from Prince of Peace Abbey, a monastery we have on the slope of Olympus Mons."

"Could you have refused?"

"Yes. Certainly. Technically you can refuse, but you really are supposed to obey. And I am the first person born and raised on Mars ever to be called to be a bishop. It would really have been unacceptable to refuse."

"How long have you been a bishop?"

"Nine years."

"So you are late getting to Rome by a few years."

"They make special dispensation for bishops this far out. We can put it off."

"So what made you decide this was the year to go?"

"No more dispensations. The pope's own secretary called to let me know."

"That sounds serious."

"I thought so," the bishop laughed as the delivery wagon bobbed and rolled along the surface toward Sakharov.

# (4.)

The wagon dropped its passengers at an airlock on the rim above the canyon town of Sakharov. An elevator took the passengers down the 350 meters to the canyon floor. A short walk through a broad tunnel and they emerged into the midst of Sakharov's busy life.

As a Martian, the bishop was used to the way the people of his planet burrowed and built underground in order to take advantage of the even temperatures and the natural radiation shielding. But Sakharov was not like this. It was much more "outdoors" than most Martian towns, contained almost entirely under gelglass within a tributary canyon.

The top of the canyon and its open end were completely sealed under an impressive, hyper-modern metal and gelglass structure. At the canyon's open end, one could look through the gelglass far down into the Valles Marineris, the enormous scar across the middle of Mars, and one of the largest canyons on any known world.

This must be what attracted the hikers.

The town itself was industrial looking, and bustling. As many as eight thousand people called it home. They lived mostly in the canyon walls and in the five- and six-story apartment buildings that jostled for space around a central lake. The lake was a few hundred meters across and constructed to look natural to the canyon, though, of course, there had not been standing surface water on Mars for millions of years.

Second shift was about to begin, and the city bustled with people heading home or heading to work.

Someday, the bishop imagined, the great canyon that lay outside Sakharov would be covered and pressurized and populated by people who would marvel at how cramped the old Martian towns were.

The Valles Marineris was big enough to house millions of people if ever it was covered and filled with atmosphere. But that would take money and time and, for all the bishop knew, engineering skills that were not yet available.

"Our scrammy leaves in five hours," David Elsman said to the bishop, who startled slightly, not having realized that the professor stayed with him after they emerged from the tunnel.

From the delivery wagon the bishop had been able to see a port with eight or ten dirigibles on a ridge above the town. The port had been too far away to see the scram jets that drop from the dirigibles. One of those would be their ride to the Frank Sinatra.

"Not enough time to enjoy Sakharov fully," the bishop said as he surveyed the gelglass several hundred meters above.

The bishop found himself wondering why he had let the Wild West reputation of the place keep him from making his way out here before. He realized, now that he was here, that he had merely swallowed the general sense of danger attached to the place and its rough-and-tumble inhabitants.

"I should have overcome that," the bishop thought. "This place is stunning," he said aloud.

"It is rather a surprise, isn't it?" David said. "It certainly gives me a better impression of Martian living than I got from Hayes."

"It does at that," the bishop said. "I have lived on Mars my whole life and have somehow missed this."

As the two strolled absently toward the lake, the bishop was taken by a sudden enthusiasm. "I saw an ad on the delivery wagon for a saloon claiming to have the best burgers on Mars," he said. "I've got a priest-friend here in town. I'll call him to meet us, and it will be my treat."

"I've never been one to turn down a free meal," David said, catching the bishop's enthusiasm.

Because the canyon in which Sakharov was built was a tributary, it sloped downward toward the great Valles Marineris. The saloon was near the bottom of the town, not far from the gelglass wall that looked down into the great canyon.

Despite the afternoon sun, much of the Marineris Valley was hidden in darkness. Even right up against the gelglass, it was impossible to see all the way to the bottom. But those parts that were visible shone brown and red and black.

The sight lifted the spirits of the traveling companions, who arrived at the saloon ready to feast on burgers and beer.

Father Van der Walt, however, turned out to be something of a wet blanket.

He was a worker priest who dressed in overalls, boots, and a rugby shirt. He greeted the bishop heartily enough, not at all one of those timid priests who fusses over a visiting bishop. And he seemed entirely comfortable sharing a burger and a beer in a mining-town saloon.

But, though he remained polite, he showed little interest in David Elsman. Rather, he seemed to want to keep bringing the conversation back around to the bishop and what he might find in Rome, given what he kept referring to as "the crisis in the Church."

At first, the bishop was happy enough to listen to the good father's concerns. David even managed to join in on the conversation by sharing some of his own observations about Church leaders he had met or read about.

All agreed that Archbishop McConnell from Glasgow had been too chummy with the New Fascists, and that it was troubling that the pope had not moved to silence the noisome prelate. But even the winning of this agreement from his dinner companions did not satisfy Father Van der Walt, who, it must be noted, was enjoying a good amount of beer with his burger.

"The pope might be one of them," he said, holding up the palms of his hands to the bishop as if to beg him not to shoot. "This new order, The Cohort of the Church Militant, the pope has been very solicitous of them, and they are tied up with the Fascists in a thousand different ways."

The bishop tolerated this talk, though he did not like it. If priests did not feel free to speak their minds, the bishop would never know what was on their minds.

The bishop did not share father's conspiratorial concerns, however. In fact, he had never been one to follow Church politics closely, thinking little good could come of it.

Earth was far away, and on Mars little reference was ever made to any of this—even among pious Catholics. Martian people still saw themselves as pioneers, as a people who were quite literally building a new world. The bishop's work in ministry had, therefore, been generally straightforward. The people needed to be reminded to look beyond the accumulation of wealth and the preoccupation with work. He called his busy flock to lift their eyes and come to the One who loves them.

He bothered very little with the grandiose politics that seemed ever to be convulsing Earth. The Fascists and the New Progressivists and the various other political factions were struggling over the meaning of life, and trying to construct systems and institutions that reflected their particular visions. The people of Mars were in a much more immediate political stage. They were trying to have enough oxygen and water and space to go on making the one thing they truly love— money.

It might be the root of all evil, but at least it was an easy evil to diagnose.

It was when people had plenty of money that they began devising great, subtle, and devious new historical projects. The evils hidden in these were often hard to diagnose and almost impossible to convince people to resist.

Perhaps this was another reason that the bishop had for so long put off the trip to Earth.

He listened politely to Father Van der Walt, and did not try to correct him. For all the bishop knew, he might be right. He did not know what he would find among the clergy of Earth.

But Mars was not Earth, and the big problems that the pope had to deal with often had little application here.

# (5.)

With every meter the dirigible rose, the bishop's anxiety increased. He was rolling rosary beads between his fingers, applying real force, but finding it impossible to settle down and pray.

"This is a stupid way to travel," he lectured himself. He thought of the pope in Rome and momentarily had no patience for the old man. Easy for him to say that it is time to come to Earth. Did the pope have to suffer the indignities of unregistered travel?

The dirigible would rise to nearly 20,000 meters using four large fans that, even in the thin Martian atmosphere, would assist the lift from the planet's surface. The scrammy would then drop about 3,000 meters, nose down, before its engines could fire. Its speed would then increase, shooting them, as they say, faster than a bullet. In a moment, the computers would turn the nose up, crushing the passengers into their seats and hurling them toward space. When they were high up and going fast, a rocket motor would fire for just under a minute and set them on a glide path toward the Frank Sinatra's rendezvous point.

None of this plan appealed to the bishop.

He knew that scrammy travel was about as safe as any other mode of travel, but the thought comforted him almost not at all. However safe it may be, it was barbaric.

His breath was short now, and shallow. His gut tightened and his head grew light.

A red light came on. A little groan of panic escaped him.

He did not want to do this. For a moment, he regretted everything, every choice he had ever made, because it all led to this.

A loud clang of metal and the nose of the scrammy dropped. The jet hung below the dirigible in that ridiculous nose-down position for several seconds. The bishop had just enough time to note the discomfort of his entire weight resting against his restraints when there was a second clang of metal and the scrammy dropped.

The panic was unbearable. The bishop's mind was blank with terror. The fall went on and on and on, until it seemed that something must have gone catastrophically wrong.

The jet had failed to fire.

This was the moment before death.

He squirmed as his body tried to prepare itself for impact.

And then, in an instant and a roar, he was pressed back into his seat, the jet's speed increasing wildly.

The turn was not at all gradual. He was suddenly pressed down hard into his seat and then into the back of his seat, which, though uncomfortable, was the first comforting thing that had happened since the red light went on.

The scrammy was rising.

The bishop began breathing again, and tears rolled back into his ears. Whether of fear or of regret, he was not certain.

He was leaving Mars.

# (6.)

The Frank Sinatra was a second-class transport, but, having no first-class experience to compare it to, the bishop did not experience it as second-class at all. Standing on the main deck, he had the feeling of standing in a broad, finely furnished tunnel that sloped rather sharply upward in both directions.

Every bit of the ship seemed designed to bestow a sense of cleanliness, efficiency, openness.

An orientation given to passengers as they assembled on the space station rendezvous point had painted a clear picture of the ship's layout: a ring that spun around a rocket in order to produce artificial gravity. The habitation ring was divided into four public areas alternating with four cabin areas. What the orientation meeting had not been able to convey was the Frank Sinatra's sense of comfort and style.

She was one of nine ships, all the same layout, that carried interplanetary passengers for the Scoundrel Line, the largest—and proudest— unregistered line in the solar system. The orientation presenter had seemed particularly proud that the line was about to grow to eleven ships, with the launch of the Ned Kelly and the Mick Jagger.

At the Sinatra's on-board check-in desk, a shiny young hologram greeted the bishop. She was pleasant and efficient and she assigned a little robot to see him to his room.

The robot led him across the lobby of the main deck and through a doorway—not a hatch—into the nearest cabin section. Once through the door, the sense of elegance and spaciousness diminished considerably, but did not altogether disappear. The cabin section felt like what one expected on a transport ship, with doors on each side of a long hallway.

The bishop nodded and said hello to a passenger here and there, and he followed the little robot through another door and another public space, this one set up for dining. A few of the early-arriving passengers were seated at white-clothed tables, but most of the room's seats were empty.

Once across the dining room, the little robot led him through another door to another hallway. The row of cabins was exactly like the last except that it was in an aqua color scheme, where the earlier had been in browns and beiges.

This made sense, as a method for telling the sections apart.

Six doors down on the right the robot stopped. It spun on little wheels to address the bishop. "Your cabin, sir. Will there be anything else?"

"No, thank you."

The bishop was always polite with robots. He knew that they had no real intelligence, and certainly no feelings, but he found that if he skimped on his manners with them, he sooner or later skimped with people, as well.

The robot rolled away, and the bishop asked his comcom implant to open the door.

The door slid open.

When he was a child, before he had gotten the comcom implant, one of his uncles used to entertain him by projecting a checker board. The two of them would play for hours, and the child would tell his uncle how he couldn't wait to get the implant, because then he would know the answer to everything.

His uncle had explained that it didn't really work that way. But, like so many children, he had thought then that the implant was something magical. Adults who had it could call up information instantly, could project images, and could communicate with one another at any distance.

Every now and then, even as a middle-aged man, the bishop got a hint of the childhood enchantment of the implant. He got such an intimation now, as he entered the unfamiliar room and the comcom set the lights as he favored, adjusted the air temperature to the coolness he preferred, and had the utility bar pour him a glass of ice-cold water.

The bishop settled in to a comfortable chair to read his breviary. After praying, he found the chair so comfortable that he nodded off for a half-hour or so until a gentle alarm sounded.

This had been explained to him at the orientation. The ship would give a series of alarms before beginning the acceleration away from Mars. The first alarm simply told passengers to prepare for departure in two hours.

Passengers were to stow their belongings and report to seats in the public areas. When the bishop reported, he found the dining area transformed. From out of the floor, or maybe brought in by robots, acceleration lounges had appeared. They were chaises that could fit themselves snugly to the body. They were also able to cocoon the user almost instantaneously should an accident occur. The headrest of each chaise was set within a white half-dome. Inside this, the user had access to telecommunications and media.

The bishop selected a lounge and got comfortable. He felt suddenly quite alone with his vision restricted by the head covering. He took a deep breath and readied himself mentally for departure and the long trip to Earth. At the moment he had no media options. All channels were set to training materials offering graphically detailed explanations of what was about to happen.

Robots would see that each passenger was accounted for and properly secured in an acceleration lounge. They would, at the same time, fully secure the ship, including each cabin. When the all clear sounded, a ten-minute count would begin. During the count, the ship's habitation ring would stop its rotation and weightlessness would ensue. The acceleration lounges, each cradling a well-secured passenger, would rotate, bringing the passengers into position for the movement of the ship, and then, after a final alarm, the high-acceleration plasma engine would fire.

This would press the passengers into their seats with a force about equal to the gravitational force on Earth. At the end of the firing of the engines, the ship would be moving at a speed that would get them to Earth in just thirty-six days.

The bishop relaxed as the robots and the ship followed each step meticulously. The ten-minute countdown ticked away, and he felt none of the anxiety he had felt while waiting to drop from the dirigible.

When the engine fired, there was no sound. The acceleration felt profoundly civilized in comparison to the dare-devilry of the scram jet.

The Frank Sinatra's one-G press was not at all bothersome. He closed his eyes and tried to imagine himself on Earth.

It struck him as funny that thousands of generations of humanity had lived and died hardly thinking about "weight" or "mass" or "gravity" at all, but—because he had lived his life on a world that was no more than a red dot in the sky to all those generations—such concepts were never far from his thinking.

All his life he had taken supplements and performed specialized exercises just so that his bone and organ systems would develop properly, which is to say, as they would develop on Earth.

And now, in his acceleration lounge, the weight of Earth did not feel bad to him. He closed his eyes and rested languorously, as a child might on the body of its mother.

# (7.)

There was not much to do on the Earth-bound ship, at least not much that appealed to the bishop.

He could read, of course, and did so for a few hours each day. And he kept up communications with his staff on Mars.

Seventeen Catholics on the ship responded to a post he put up on the Sinatra's social network, and he celebrated morning Mass with them each day in a rec room.

Only two were from the Diocese of Mars, the others all travelers returning to Earth from various projects or excursions. Most seemed pleased and impressed to find themselves traveling with a bishop, and he spent a good deal of time with couples and little groups for meals.

But his most frequent visit was with a Mormon family—the Asantes—because they offered a rare skill that he valued very highly; they knew how to play whist. It was a game he had been playing since his days as a deacon ministering in detention facilities. But it was unusual to find people who enjoyed the game as much as he.

He ran into David Elsman on the second day of the journey, and Elsman was cordial. He was dining at a table of six young people—perhaps students returning to school from a year abroad or some such adventure. Four of the six were young women, who seemed to be entirely taken by David's charms.

The bishop stopped by their table just long enough to get David's agreement to dine together soon, before excusing himself to make a whist game.

But he and David did not dine together nor run into one another for more than a week. With some concern, the bishop finally placed a call to David's cabin.

"David, how is the journey treating you?" the bishop asked even before David stepped into frame. When he did, the bishop could see instantly that the trip was not treating him well at all.

The young man hardly seemed the elegant and blithe conversationalist whose company had been so enjoyable. He was dressed in what appeared to be old exercise clothes, his professorial mane of hair was unkempt, and his eyes were puffy.

"I'm sorry bishop, but I am a bit out of ... I have not been able to sleep."

"Oh, I'm very sorry."

The bishop once had an insomniac priest who suffered terribly and required a surprisingly intensive medical intervention. "Do you suffer insomnia regularly?"

"No," David said with a kind of little boy shrug and wince.

The bishop waited a moment, thinking more was forthcoming. But no more was said. "How about we go for a stroll or have a cup of tea together?" he asked.

"Um ... I think I'll pass for now," David said tiredly. "I have some ... just some work I want to get to. Thank you, though."

With that the link closed, and the bishop found himself staring thoughtfully at a holo of the Frank Sinatra's logo and the words, "Would you like to place another call?"

He got a note the next day from David, saying that he was getting ShipDoc care and was feeling a little better. "Be in touch as soon as ShipDoc is done with me," the note ended, apparently cheerfully.

With some of his concerns for David settled, the bishop set off for another engagement to play whist.

He was greeted at the door by an eight-year-old—one of the youngest of the Asante's five children.

"I think we might not be playing cards tonight," the child reported, "but come on in. I'm not sure."

The Asante family had a suite of three adjoining cabins, which were always neat and welcoming in that very middle-class African way. The Asante parents were both PhDs from Mwanza Polytechnic Institute, and this family trip had been at least partly business, as they helped construct power units for a Mormon station colony. The family was close and seemed happy, always challenging one another in games, or sharing music, or just laughing together.

The usual sounds of singing and game playing were absent from the little warren of Asante cabins tonight, however. And the quiet was unnerving. The child led the bishop into the family's common area.

The bishop caught the Asantes unawares for a moment, sitting alone at the table, facing each other closely across one corner, and locked in some quietly passionate back and forth.

Had they been arguing?

He could not tell.

"Oh, bishop," Mrs. Asante said when she saw him. "I am very sorry, we had forgotten about cards tonight."

"Please, come sit down," Mr. Asante said.

"I can come another time," the bishop answered as he kept just beyond the threshold of the room, "you are a busy family."

The Asantes would not hear of it, however, and insisted that he sit while they made tea.

They made no effort to locate a deck of cards or to seek a game partner for him among their children. Instead, when the tea was ready, they joined him at the table and seemed to fumble for what to say.

The bishop decided that directness was the best course and asked as gently as he could whether anything was wrong.

Mr. Asante rubbed his forehead as if troubled over what to say, but Mrs. Asante looked the bishop in the eye.

"We have noticed an anomaly," Mrs. Asante told him, "with the ship."

"An anomaly?"

"We get messages from Earth each day," Mr. Asante said.

"They are time-stamped, of course," Mrs. Asante continued her husband's thought as if the two had decided to take turns. The bishop always liked when husbands and wives did this little trick.

"And the stamps are incorrect," Mr. Asante took his turn. "We checked the communications charts, and today Mars is a 7.43 minute delay from Earth. But the timestamp for today reads 8.07 minutes."

"We are getting farther away from Earth?" the bishop asked.

The Asantes nodded.

"Well, maybe the route we are taking...," the bishop began, but then stopped. There was no point in finishing the thought. There is no "route" to Earth that takes one out beyond Mars.

"Where are we headed?" the bishop asked gravely.

"Without triangulating, it is impossible to be sure, but we ran some simulations," Mr. Asante said. "Now, you understand, there is no way to be certain—"

"Ceres," Mrs. Asante interrupted. "We are almost certainly headed for Ceres."

# (8.)

The Asante children, it turned out, had been encouraged to find quiet activities for the evening: reading or media or muted card games in their bunks. Still, the bishop was sensitive to their proximity, and now that the conversation had turned to Ceres, he spoke in hushed tones.

"We will have to alert the Fleet," he all but whispered.

"This is an unregistered ship," Mr. Asante reminded him. "Will the Fleet even care where we are headed?"

"If Ceres is part of the conversation, I think they will take an interest."

"We have had a few hours to talk this over already, bishop," Mrs. Asante said. "We are thinking we should call the Scoundrel Lines and see if they have a clue what is going on. Then we can call the Fleet if we do not get a satisfactory answer. Also, we need to gather the passengers and explain this. Everyone has a right to know, and maybe someone has helpful information."

"We cannot go to Ceres," Mr. Asante said, seeming to speak to his own folded hands as they rest on the table in front of him. "I do not want my children taken there, even if it means disabling this ship."

"Yes, of course," the bishop said, "but have either of you got any clue why we seem to be headed there? What could this be about?"

"There have been rumors of war," Mrs. Asante offered, though it seemed not really to explain anything.

"We are being kidnapped," Mr. Asante said. "Who knows why?"

"Perhaps we are to be hostages," the bishop suggested. "If that is the case, could we simply leave the ship in lifeboats and await rescue?"

"The lifeboats have very limited fuel," Mrs. Asante answered.

"But we don't need to go anywhere," the bishop countered, "we could just sit in the lifeboats and wait."

"It doesn't work that way," Mr. Asante said, seeming for a moment a little amused. "The lifeboats would need fuel to get away from the Frank Sinatra and to change their own trajectory. They don't have that kind of power. We could climb into a lifeboat right now and fire it away from the ship, but it would still be on its way to Ceres. It doesn't have enough power to change its overall direction by much. It certainly doesn't have enough power to come to a stop from the speed we are traveling. The only way to keep us from Ceres now is to fire the ship's engine. That will probably require a coded communication from the Scoundrel Line, and I am guessing that whoever has hijacked this ship has locked Scoundrel out or we would already have seen a course correction."

# (9.)

The bishop was one of the last to enter the dining hall, and he found it packed with passengers sitting on tables and chairs. There were 137 of them, the ship's full complement, except for 17 children whose parents had not let them attend.

They were here because he had sent a ship's message asking them all to attend. In the absence of a human captain, the bishop and the Asantes, because they were the first to bring the problem to the attention of other passengers, and perhaps because of some natural qualities, had been informally turned to as leaders.

There was a loud buzz of conversation in the room. The bishop had to excuse himself and squeeze between seats several times to make his way to the front where a single table was set up as if for a panel discussion.

Mr. and Mrs. Asante were members of the panel, as were a very tired-looking and wiry young man and an equally tired-looking but stylish older woman. As he reached the front of the room, the bishop asked the panel members if they were ready to go. Each nodded, though with little apparent enthusiasm.

The bishop raised his hands high over his head and wide apart, as if imparting a momentous blessing. He had to hold the pose for a moment before it did the trick, but the buzz grew quiet.

"There are a few things to report," the bishop said. "I know many of you have already heard what I have to say, but it is important to be sure that everyone has the full story.

"Henry here," he said, gesturing to the wiry young man, "has been able to establish a stable link with Scoundrel officials. The ship did not put up much opposition. It only seems interested in blocking communications related to navigation and a few other limited areas. The technicians of the Scoundrel Line have reported to us that they believe they are locked out of the navigation computer manually. That is to say, someone has sabotaged the hardware of the ship. There are two possibilities for this. One is that the ship was sabotaged before we left the orbit of Mars, and the other is that it was sabotaged by one of us before the ship fired the plasma rocket."

The bishop waited a moment before going on.

"The first question the legal people at Scoundrel Lines have insisted I ask is whether anyone would like to confess."

At this question there was a light grumble of consternation. Passengers seemed unsure whether or not the bishop was making a sick joke.

"I don't mean to be obnoxious by asking such a question, but I have been advised that in a situation like this—where the intent of our saboteur is unclear—it may well be that the person has been waiting for an opportunity to address the entire population of the ship. If that is the case, I offer that person the opportunity to come forward now."

There was a swiveling of heads, but no one came forward.

"Fine, that is done," the bishop said. "Given that no one has stepped forward, the most likely scenario is that Ceres is our destination and we will not know why we have been diverted until we get there. Now for the reports from the ad-hoc committee."

Mrs. Asante rose first. She was calm and spoke plainly. "Our options are extremely limited at this point. No ship is in position to intercept us or assist us in time to prevent us reaching Ceres. We can try to reach the navigation computer ourselves, or we can attempt to send robots to reach the computer. The problem with the first choice is that the navigation computer has sealed all hatches leading from the habitation ring to the center of the ship. The problem with the second choice has entirely to do with programming, as I will let my colleague here explain momentarily."

It took more than half an hour for the members of the panel each to make a little brief presentation and to answer questions from the passengers.

The bishop, though playing the role of moderator, found himself paying very little attention to the questions and answers.

He had been at the center of nearly all conversations between the ship, the Fleet, and the Scoundrel Line. Nothing being said so far was new to him.

His mind drifted and he began to daydream about earlier meetings from other times.

He recalled planning meetings from more than two decades ago in which he, as pastor of a small parish, had to oversee discussions about building a new parish hall. He also remembered another posting, at a community that had been celebrating Sunday Mass for years in a repair hanger; he'd had to build a parish church. And then there was the time that his associate pastor had required hospitalization for drug dependency. He'd had to explain that to a room filled very much like this one.

In each of these situations, the bishop had, at some point, made up his own mind and found himself more or less waiting for others to catch up. He entertained himself in such circumstances by becoming a student of group dynamics. It seemed to him that people nearly always played roles in these kinds of meetings. They seemed to need to play roles: some helpful, some not.

There was always, for example, at least one voice, and usually a few supporting voices, taking the position that everyone else was over-complicating things.

The bishop watched as one such group developed around the notion that the Frank Sinatra's problem could be solved easily "if we would just improvise some explosives and separate the habitation ring from the plasma rocket. Let the rocket continue on to Ceres, and let the Fleet come pick us up."

No amount of explaining the physical impossibility of this plan could satisfy the "there must be a simple solution" crowd. They merely grumbled about how *it could work if we all put our heads together to make it work, but if no one is willing to try then, well...*

How many people lived and died, the bishop wondered, convinced that life had simple answers and that other people were over-complicating things?

And then there was the conspiracy group. In this case, they coalesced around the rather pointless idea that this was probably a Fleet conspiracy to discredit unregistered lines.

The bishop, for the life of him, could not figure out how repeating this theory could be thought helpful, and yet it was repeated more than once as if it held some magical explanatory power. The bishop supposed that there were just some people for whom any problem will do but the one at hand.

By far the largest group, however, was made up of those who said nothing at all.

The bishop supposed them to be reasonable and responsible enough to accept what the panel members were saying. But who could be sure? The bishop was grateful for their quiet seriousness, even if he could not say exactly what it meant.

The last presentation was by Darlene, the eldest of the panelists—a robotics expert. The bishop emerged from his scholarly detachment when she spoke. It seemed to him that reprogramming the robots to assist in some way was the most likely course of fruitful action.

But in quick fashion, Darlene doused that last hope. "There is no means of reprogramming ship robots except through the navigation computer."

She used her right index finger to draw a diagram in the air depicting how the robots interfaced. The diagram lingered there, projected by her comcom implant for the passengers to examine.

"Think of the ship itself as a single tool. The robots are part of that tool. Certainly they can act in a way that appears autonomous, but the decisions they make are based on constant updates regarding the disposition of the ship. Those updates come directly from the navigation computer. They are made to respond to the navigation computer with its multitude of sensors and internal directives. They cannot act on their own."

"That's that," the bishop told himself. He settled in for extended discussion that must now follow before the full complement of passengers would be ready to accept reality. Some few would hold out for a long time, insisting until they had exhausted the room that another answer could be found. In the end, however, reality would wear down resistance.

The Frank Sinatra was on its way to Ceres, and there was no one but the hijacker who could change that fact.

# (10.)

After the meeting, the robots restored the dining area to its clean and elegant simplicity. Meals were served on schedule; all the usual entertainment options remained. But everything was different.

The spirit of the ship had changed, and when the spirit changes, everything changes.

The bishop detected in his shipboard flock a quiet increase in seriousness at Mass. Some were afraid, that was clear. Maybe all were. But not all of the seriousness, he thought, was born of fear. The prayers simply seemed to mean more at a time like this, allowing people a greater sense of connection to them.

In many ways, the Catholic Mass, with its great variety of supplications and encouragements, is best suited to people in sadness, danger, or sickness. And when the Catholic is in such a state, the Mass is more alive than ever.

The bishop got several requests to hear confessions, and found the penitents to be sober but ultimately confident in the sacrament.

One woman asked during her confession if he thought they would be killed or tortured on Ceres. He thought only briefly about it before he realized that he really did not believe so. Had the Fascists wanted to kill them, they could simply have blown up the ship. And what purpose would torture serve?

"No," he told her, and then, thinking out loud, he said, "I suspect there is something on this ship that Ceres wants."

# (11.)

ShipDoc set off a ship-wide alarm.

A cleaning unit had found a body, and until certainty could be established about cause of death, a body found on a ship in transit was always treated as a threat. Robots immediately began accounting for each soul on the manifest.

For some reason, the alarm filled the bishop with concern for the Asantes. He tried to check on them but found it impossible to reach their cabins. The hallways were jammed with people and machines.

One of the anthropomorphic servant robots met the bishop as he was trying to work his way toward the Asantes.

"Bishop Gastelum," the robot said, "I am glad to find you alright."

"I, yes, well, I am trying to visit the Asantes." Aboard ship, one never worried whether a robot knew who you were talking about.

"Bishop, I have been asked to convey to you that—" the bishop looked around the robot, thinking he might just pick his way past "—the Frank Sinatra is currently on security check status. I cannot insist that you return to your cabin, but I must plead with you to do so. There has been an incident that requires investigation and the robot staff is simply trying to collect data, preserve evidence, and account for all passengers."

The bishop wanted to be annoyed, but he found he was not. The robot was well programmed with facial expressions and gesticulations designed to reduce tensions and garner cooperation. These programs worked remarkably well. And, anyway, what the robot was saying was entirely fair. If there had been an incident, it was reasonable that the ship would want to preserve evidence, and so on.

"Alright, sure, I understand," he told the robot. "Do you need to escort me?"

"Yes, sir, unless you object to that."

Lunch was served in the cabins, and the Frank Sinatra remained on a kind of voluntary lockdown while robots and computers finished the death investigation.

All ship's data was then sent to Scoundrel Lines' headquarters.

Whatever mechanism had taken control of the navigation systems seemed to take no interest in the death investigation. Apparently navigation was the only area that had been compromised.

When it came to meals, entertainments, cabin pressures, temperatures, deaths, death investigations, and every other non-navigation function, the ship just went about its business.

From his cabin, the bishop had been able to check in on the Asantes. All were fine.

He learned who had died in the same way the rest of the ship did, in a message from a Scoundrel Lines vice president.

The executive explained in his holo that he was the closest company official to the Frank Sinatra— visiting a station colony beyond Mars. That meant he could communicate with very little delay.

He was about the bishop's age and addressed the ship from what looked like a library. He wore a blue coat over a white shirt with no tie. And though he seemed well trained in corporate spokesmanship, he mercifully did not rely on it. Instead, he spoke calmly and apparently sincerely.

"A cleaning unit found a young passenger, Professor David Elsman from Oxford University, hanging in his room this morning, apparently a suicide," the official said. "ShipDoc was unable to revive him. I know you are all going through a great deal of stress at the moment, and I am truly sorry about the alarms and the ship security routines. It's all pre-programmed stuff that allows us to ensure passenger safety while we also ensure that data and evidence are preserved."

The vice president went on in that vein for a few more minutes and then took questions from passengers.

The bishop heard no more of it, however. He turned his holo off and fell to his knees at the edge of the bed.

# (12.)

"The extremely low gravity of the dwarf planet Ceres allows, in an odd way, for high gravity living," Mr. Asante explained to the bishop. "Each of the three main population centers is a wide, sub-surface drum on an enormous axel. The spin of these drums on their axels is fast enough to create the equivalent of the gravity on Earth as the people inside the drums are pressed against the drum's inner walls. It works exactly the way this ship's habitation ring works, but on a massive scale. Such a project would be impossible on Earth, or even on Mars, because the real gravity of those planets would interfere with the artificial gravity created by the spin. Cerean gravity is so weak that it does not create anything more than negligible interference."

"I think this has all been explained to me at one time or another." The bishop served himself some salad from the big wooden—he assumed African—bowl. "But I am one of those people who live among all these technologies without ever remembering much about how they work. I'm afraid I simply take it all for granted."

"Technology works best when it is invisible," Mr. Asante said.

Ceres had begun communicating with the Frank Sinatra a few days earlier, and had relayed a very precise set of instructions regarding what would happen once the ship reached the dwarf planet.

Among those instructions was a request that upon arrival Bishop Mark Gastelum come immediately to meet with the Fuhrer. While that meeting was taking place, all other passengers were to wait on the ship.

The bishop was not sure why he had been selected. Perhaps there was, indeed, a fascist spy on the ship who had relayed to Ceres the informal leadership role that the bishop had taken on aboard the Sinatra since the discovery by the Asantes that the ship was headed to Ceres. Perhaps the Fascists remembered the bishop's moment of publicity after he tried to book UNAC passage and thought of him as a man they might be able to deal with.

Whatever was the case, the other passengers saw no reason to argue with this "request" of the Fascists, nor could the bishop think of any reason to refuse.

"How are you feeling about meeting the Fuhrer?" Mrs. Asante asked.

"I don't know," he said. "Part of me wants to be defiant, show some bravado and all that—"

"Ah, very Christ-like," Mr. Asante teased.

"Exactly," the bishop laughed.

"You will be fine," Mrs. Asante said, as if to settle an argument. "You do not have to act like Jesus. You have to let Jesus be Jesus. Isn't he alive in you?"

The bishop blushed slightly at this reminder, "Very good point."

"What else can you do? Jesus told us to love others, we love others," Mr. Asante offered philosophically.

The bishop stared quietly at Mr. Asante for a moment, making an interior attempt to love the Fuhrer. He would have to work on it.

Mrs. Asante went on explaining the technical details of Cerean communities, but seemed grumpy doing so.

"I do not like to give credit to these people," she admitted to the bishop, "but it is difficult to explain what they have built without being impressed."

The bishop had been studying New Fascist history ever since word had come that the Fuhrer requested a meeting with him.

"The cities of Ceres probably could not have been built by anyone but the Fascists," he insisted to Mrs. Asante. He had come to feel that their great engineering accomplishments should not be denied, but should be put in the context of the brutality with which they got things done.

"They first drove all competing settlements off Ceres, and then they enforced a harsh discipline on their own people as they put all of their economic and industrial power into building the rotating cities."

Mrs. Asante grunted at that and continued describing what she knew about life on Ceres from her studies. In fact, she had read a good deal about them to keep abreast of the latest advances in settlement power systems, her area of expertise.

"In many ways, the Cerean cities represent the most Earth-like living situation yet created off Earth. The Cerean people live 'outdoors' in massive, full-gravity environments. And they have all the resources of a planet with which to keep building and expanding," she explained.

"Their children are naturally healthy. They are protected by the watery surface of Ceres from radiation, and they require no special treatments to combat the ill effects of low gravity living. They do not spend their lives floating through locks and closing hatches behind them."

*Lebensraum*, the bishop thought.

The word—recalled from his recent studies—appeared unbidden in his consciousness. It meant something like "breathing room" as he recalled. It seemed that one of the common traits of fascism, whether new or old, was the dream of wide open space in which to breed a humanity incapable of anything but glorious victories, one after another.

# (13.)

The lack of significant gravity on Ceres—just a fraction of one percent of that on Earth—meant the Frank Sinatra could land, because "landing" on Ceres was more like docking, and the ship would have no trouble pulling away when—or if—it was time to leave.

Four grim-faced and black-clad Fascist soldiers, the swastika with red-claws displayed on their *de rigueur* armbands, came aboard to escort the bishop.

As he had tried to learn all he could about the Fuhrer and about the movement that had so upset the solar system, he found that the Frank Sinatra's library—otherwise all but comprehensive—was missing a film of particular interest. The ship had to search the Web to find a copy.

The ship's media computer asked the bishop on three separate occasions whether he was sure this was the film he was looking for.

"Yes," the bishop said each time, almost expecting the media lounge to sigh its disapproval.

*The Triumph of the Vanguard* was a propaganda work, based on some primitive propaganda produced by the old Fascists.

The holo-film began with the image of a ship descending upon a white and blue planet, Ceres. The curve of the planet was short, but the blues and whites of the surface were stunning.

Soon the ship came upon a settlement—a port. Cranes and docking towers with military ships gave a sense that something commanding had been willed into existence on this forbidding little world a hundred million miles from Earth.

A colossal surface crane captured the incoming ship and deposited it gently on a massive service elevator.

The holo showed the windows of the port's various buildings filled with happy faces, cheering faces, all ecstatic at the coming of this one, small ship. The straight-arm victory salute was offered everywhere with an enthusiasm bordering on mania.

The elevator descended into blackness and emerged into the bright, clean space of one of the rotating-drum cities.

The small ship emerged from the elevator and flew out into the drum city, landing in an open field where it was greeted by a massive crowd. The vessel's side door opened and the Fuhrer stepped out. He was greeted with wild eruptions of "Heil, Heil, Heil!"

The lesser Fascist leadership followed him out of the ship, each offering a one-armed salute to the crowd.

Scene after scene of marching and goose-stepping and weaponry on parade followed, always returning to shots of the Fuhrer, his left hand gripping his belt with theatrical virility and his right hand raised in salute.

In their own way, the images were mesmerizing and deeply attractive.

The bishop found himself surrounded by the holo-images of healthy women with flowers in their braided hair. The men and children were as bright-eyed as scouts, as hale as Arthurian knights.

The holo gave the bishop a powerful sense of emersion into the actual event, and the bishop was reminded again why so many people became addicted to the holos, often taking V-nano to heighten the experience. This combination of altered brains and life-like media left many young people convinced that reality was insufficient. It could no longer be enough. Augmented reality, as they called it, was the only life worth living. Watching this holo-film now, he could see the allure.

And he could feel the special allure of this particular film. It showed a society with an orderliness and vigor that contrasted deeply—and favorably—with the wildness and self-centeredness of the prevalent culture that had flung itself, seemingly without purpose, onto planets, moons, asteroids, and station colonies around the solar system.

These energetic Fascists loved an ideal, and it was not an entirely grotesque ideal. There was something about their shared purpose, their order, and their vitality that testified convincingly.

The romance of the Fascist vision was real.

Then came the Fuhrer's speech.

It was delivered in a huge hall before thousands upon thousands of uniformed men and women, where banners resembling old Roman legionary regalia were marched in, followed by swastika flags, and then a few other forms of regalia that the bishop did not recognize.

The Fuhrer's growling voice demanded a kind of moral perfection of the vanguard. Those who were too soft must be weeded out, for it was the steely brutality of the vanguard that would rescue humanity from its paralysis, its debauchery.

Perhaps he was getting old, but the bishop could hardly comprehend why anyone would attribute depth or power to the Fuhrer's ideas. It was all vague talk of "strength" and "will" and "purity" that rested on nothing.

Far more interesting were the images, regalia, marching, and shouting. Such pageantry—along with the Fuhrer's dramatic delivery—gave insipid thinking a bold aura, even on holo-film.

The building in which the Fuhrer addressed his elites could well have been a church, and—though they were militant and rough—the elements of pageantry could just as well be called a liturgy as a rally.

Alone in his media lounge, the bishop flushed a little when the Fuhrer described the movement: "In its entity it will be like a religious order."

# (14.)

Getting to the Fuhrer took a good deal of walking, and the bishop was certain this was intentional. From the Frank Sinatra, he had been brought down an elevator with a padded ceiling and floor. Gravity was so low here that the padding was necessary. Passengers who did not slip their feet into the straps bolted to the floor "floated" up against the ceiling.

The bishop was not sure how fast the elevator descended nor how deep into the dwarf planet it took him, but he supposed it must have been several kilometers to the bottom of the shaft.

When the doors opened, he found himself looking out onto a most improbable sight. He was at one end of the city's axel, and the city of New Nuremburg spun before him.

The view was incredible in both its simple beauty and in its extreme oddity. An entire Earth city—he supposed the look must be German—had been constructed on the inside of a two-kilometer-wide barrel. The floor he stood on was transparent. He could see the great axle turning beneath his feet and, in front of him, the great spokes extending out to the edges of the barrel.

The barrel's inner curve was covered with homes, business districts, grassy parks, hills, and even little rivers and ponds. The axle crossed right through the middle of the "sky" of this city, and it was ingenious. The entire length of it was covered with a blue luminescent surface that lit everything below. The bishop was to find out later that it was on a 24-hour clock, and mimicked the colors of a northern European sky throughout the day and night. It radiated the full spectrum of the sun's light.

The bishop had seen many artificial skies in the subterranean towns on Mars, but none as inspired as this.

Directly across from him, the bishop could see the other end of the axle as it extended into the planet itself. From that side of the axle he could see fully how the great spokes protruded.

He was ushered into another elevator that made its way down the inner wall of one of the spokes. It descended slowly, allowing the bishop a long time to contemplate the beauty and genius of this New Nuremberg. And as the elevator got lower, the sense of "gravity" grew heavier and heavier.

He had been advised to take a nasal spray to prevent sickness as he made the transition to the full spin at the floor of the city. The spray helped, and the bishop felt little of the queasiness that usually accompanied such events.

At the bottom, he stepped out onto the "ground" of New Nuremberg and felt a heaviness equivalent to Earth gravity.

He also felt a lightness of elation.

"This is the closest humans have come to replicating Earth on another planet," he reminded himself. Even the motifs of eagles and swastikas could not rob the city of its disarming beauty.

His escorts rushed him to a waiting car, which cruised silently through streets lined with triple-deck houses surrounded by fences and flower gardens. Beyond this area of housing, the car passed through a business district with small shops and theaters and beer halls. The street then became a boulevard that led down a row of titanic government buildings. The car skirted the edge of an enormous public square. At the end of this loomed—there could be no other word for it—the Chancellery.

It was gray stone, both dark and monumental.

The bishop was escorted up its sweeping front steps and through a pair of gigantic doors that swung open for him. Inside, he passed through three halls. The first was the main entry hall, which was in every way constructed to dwarf whoever crossed its long, and apparently real, marble floors. The floors were so highly polished that the bishop worried about slipping.

The walls were stone and maybe twenty meters high. The colors were heavy blacks and grays. On a different scale, the room could have been a mausoleum.

Halfway across this massive and echoing hall, his escorts stopped and motioned for him to continue on through the next doors on his own.

These, too, were massive, and crossing to them alone gave the bishop an alarming sense of vulnerability. The sounds of his shoes on the floor seemed almost a summons to whatever evil might lie hidden nearby.

The second hall was warmer. Its walls were a deep brown and highly polished wood, with tapestries hung at intervals. The floor was carpeted with an enormous but finely woven beige carpet inlaid with medieval-looking pastoral and floral scenes.

Here and there were finely crafted wooden chairs in groups of four. Their presence—which seemed tiny in this great space—emphasized the grandeur of the setting.

The bishop walked alone through this hall, and passed into the third, which was smaller and more businesslike. Across this smaller hall were two rich brown wooden doors. To the side of each door stood a soldier, hand lance pistol on the hip.

In front of the soldiers were two desks that faced each other, and at each desk sat a middle-aged woman doing what appeared to be secretarial work.

One of these secretaries motioned for the bishop to take a seat on a fine leather bench by her desk.

When he sat, she stood and exited through the doors, which the soldiers drew open for her.

A moment later she emerged and sat at her desk.

The bishop tried, with mixed success, to resist the sense of insignificance his hosts so clearly wanted him to feel.

At an invisible signal, the soldiers opened the doors again and the Fuhrer stood in the doorway, his arms crossed in front of him.

He was dressed in drab green though neatly pressed military uniform with no coat. At his side was a pistol.

"Bishop Gastelum," he said, "please come in."

The bishop rose to greet him, and the Fuhrer shook his hand with masculine formality.

The office within was another great cavern of highly polished and inlaid brown wood. Its windows were floor to ceiling, and they looked out upon the city. In front of them was a great marble table adorned with an enormous arrangement of flowers.

To the left was a finely crafted brown desk.

To the right was a sitting area with a blue couch and matching chairs.

The bulk of the office, however, was a great open carpeted area.

Vast and impersonal interior spaces seemed to be a key element of the Fascist aesthetic.

At the center of this carpet, two comfortable leather chairs sat facing each other.

It was to these that the Fuhrer invited the bishop.

"Thank you for coming," he said as he directed the bishop to one of the chairs. "Let us sit together and talk comfortably."

As he said these words, the soldiers closed the great brown doors and left them alone.

# (15.)

Joseph Hadamar was an average-looking man of average height. He had dark hair and a medium build and, despite his reputation for violence, he looked like he would be more at home in an insurance office than in a street fight.

He was not at all average, however, in his bearing.

The bishop had often heard him described as mesmerizing, and there was something fascinating about him. The man strode, his look challenged, he seemed not so much to be present as to be presenting himself. And yet he had a strangely disinterested air about him, as if—despite all the obviously studied presentation of himself—he was not really invested in the moment.

The bishop reminded himself that this man, whatever he might appear, really was a street fighter. He had been in prison for his beliefs, he had killed for them, and his stride had, in just two decades of public life, become a stride across history.

Millions saw him as the virile embodiment of a new movement, a refreshment of the tired and bored human spirit. Millions more saw him as a barbarian.

"You are a man of action," he said to the bishop, as if this judgment were something really to be valued. "I have reports of how you took charge and brought civility when others became uncivilized."

"You mean on the ship?" the bishop asked, startled by the statement. Perhaps the Fuhrer was under the impression that the one thing every conversation needed was the quick expression of his own judgment. Perhaps this was how it was when you were the Fuhrer—people simply waited for your word.

The Fuhrer did not answer but held the bishop's eye sternly, evenly.

"Well, there was not much action to take," the bishop said. "The ship was going where it was going."

The Fuhrer smiled.

"Exactly," he said. "The first duty of a leader is to admit reality."

The bishop had often thought the same thing himself, which was unnerving, and left him unsure how to reply.

"I had noted your earlier attempt to book passage on a UNAC ship," the Fuhrer said.

"Well, you can see how that went," the bishop answered, attempting humor.

"But you knew how it would go when you applied," the Fuhrer said. "I admired your willingness to face the ridicule that comes when one exposes an injustice."

In fact, that was exactly what had happened. As much as the bishop had told himself that the whole episode was just foolishness, he had applied for passage on a UNAC ship both because he thought he might slip through and because he was annoyed at the injustice of the travel ban. The Fuhrer was no fool.

"Perhaps it was a useless gesture," the bishop offered.

"A bothersome gesture to the arrogant," the Fuhrer countered. "I have found it is rarely useless to bother the arrogant."

"But my job is to love," the bishop said without thinking, in fact, without knowing exactly where the words had come from. Perhaps Mrs. Asante.

At this the Fuhrer smiled broadly. "Yes," he said, "humanity has forgotten how to love what is good, what is healthy, what is lively and beautiful. I imagine we could have great conversations about love. You are perhaps surprised that I am so enthusiastic on this topic, but I am a Christian—a Positive Christian. I believe in all that is wholesome and healthy of Christ. The New Reich is entirely about love."

The bishop knew from his studies what the New Reich was about, but there seemed little point in challenging the Fuhrer on his understanding of love. "I have always found love to be a struggle. It is not easy to give oneself to others as Jesus did."

The Fuhrer did not take the bait. The bishop knew that in the Fascist understanding of Jesus, there was no such thing as giving oneself. Jesus had been crucified by those who were not able to accept his teaching—which was about the superiority of those who follow their own will against the corrupting influence of the weak who conspire against beauty and individuality.

Instead of replying to the bishop's subtle challenge, however, the Fuhrer closed off the conversation with another of his summary judgments. "A great many lies have been told about Jesus," he said without explanation.

"May I ask a question?" the bishop said. He leaned back in his chair and crossed his legs. "Have we been brought here as hostages?"

The bishop's attempt to change the tone had no effect on the Fuhrer. He studied the bishop, seeming to pass no judgment at all, seeming not to care one way or another what the bishop thought.

"You are not hostages. We redirected your ship in order to make an arrest, but our opportunity to seize the spy has passed, so this episode is essentially over. I have asked you here to convey our apologies for inconveniencing you, to ask you to convey to your fellow passengers that anyone who would like to remain on Ceres is welcome to for as long as they like, and that those who would like to resume their travels immediately may do so. As a courtesy, the Reich will pay for all travel expenses and will include some token of restoration for the difficulty our arrest attempt has caused."

With this the Fuhrer stood and offered his hand to the bishop, who stood and shook it.

"Thank you," the bishop said, a bit nonplussed by the immediacy of the dismissal

"A pleasure," the Fuhrer said, and he strode off toward his desk. Some hidden signal had been given; the soldiers opened the doors.

The bishop left a bit flustered. David Elsman was a spy?

# (16.)

No escorts awaited the bishop outside the Chancellery. He was on his own to do as he liked. Perhaps they were watching him, but for what reason? What could he possibly matter to them?

He tried to think through what the Fuhrer had just said. Perhaps the Fascists were searching the Frank Sinatra for anything David had left behind, but even they must know that they would find nothing. If David really was a spy, he would have destroyed anything of value to them before he killed himself.

The bishop now got a clearer understanding of David's last days. He must have known that the ship had been diverted. Knowing he was trapped, he'd taken his own life to protect whatever secrets he was carrying.

The bishop said a prayer for him and decided to take a walk before returning to the ship. There was little likelihood that he would ever again have the chance to see a Cerean city.

He headed for the district of little shops that the car had passed on the way to the Chancellery.

It was more than two hundred meters across the grand square, and the walk was uncomfortable, both because the gravity was tiring and because the square was almost entirely empty, bringing back an intense feeling of vulnerability.

Once through the square and into the business district, however, the bishop began to pass other people. They were universally friendly. Each one greeted the bishop with a smile, a "Hail, Victory," and a raised right hand. The bishop smiled and said hello, and no one seemed to take offense when he did not return the salute.

The smiling faces greeting the bishop came in every color. The New Fascists were not racists. In fact, New Fascism had become popular precisely because people saw it as correcting the errors of the original Fascism. Their new movement was rooted in a sense that Earth itself was the homeland, the motherland, and the purification she needed was not racial, but what the Fuhrer was fond of calling a "burning out of degeneracy."

As he walked the amicable streets of New Nuremberg, the bishop found it hard to think of these Fascists in villainous terms. In fact, they had a point; degeneracy—the loss of higher qualities in favor of lower—was a problem the whole of society faced. Indeed, it was the problem.

In the shop district, the bishop found many more people. Mothers walked with younger children, while older children seemed to run free through the charming little parks and squares that intermingled with the cafes, the markets, and the specialty shops selling chocolates or dresses or handmade shoes.

The bishop wandered past a chocolate shop, or rather was about to pass, when he saw a man standing inside waving to him to come in.

"We do not see many tourists," the man said when the bishop entered. "Can I offer you a sample to try?"

The man had a tray with a variety of delicate little treats.

The bishop tried a dark chocolate with almonds, and struck up a conversation with the chocolatier, who was originally from Mars, as it turned out. They exchanged pleasantries about the old home planet and its various popular spots. The bishop asked about what news they got on Ceres and was a bit surprised to find that full news access was the norm.

"We're not backwards," the chocolatier chided him gently. "Did you think we live cut off from the world?"

"I suppose I didn't know," the bishop said, "but, yes, I guess I expected ... censorship."

"I would expect more understanding from you, a Catholic," the chocolatier said, sounding not so much miffed as genuinely surprised. "You belong to a 'hate group,' do you not?"

"Ah, yes. I see your point," the bishop said without mentioning that the point was slightly problematic to him. Just because one side of the political spectrum over-used the term "hate group" didn't mean that there were no actual hate groups. "So you are saying that I have fallen for propaganda?"

"We are very alert to propaganda," the chocolatier answered. "It is used against us thousands of times every day."

"Maybe you *should* censor, then," the bishop tried to joke.

"Our belief is that strong ideas expressed with confidence win in the end. We do not censor, but we have required reading and viewing and even study sections. This keeps our minds strong and alert and able to resist propaganda. We place a great emphasis on correct thinking, healthy thinking—this is what will rescue humanity."

The bishop was about to reply that humanity had already been rescued when he was interrupted by the appearance of his uniformed escorts in the doorway to the shop.

"The Fuhrer requests your presence at 1700 hours," they told him. "Will you be on your ship at that time?" The chocolatier quickly disappeared into the back of the shop.

The bishop was flustered, but thought he managed to hide it. "I am heading there now," he said.

"We will pick you up at 16:30."

They left as abruptly as they had appeared, and now the bishop found himself alone.

He stood for a moment, staring out the window at the loveliness of the street scene—the shops, the mothers, the children.

Suddenly, he had the urge to return to Mars. The Vatican would understand. He could make the trip to Rome in another year or two. As things were, he would be absent from his diocese for almost six months even if he left Ceres right away.

"Excuse me," the chocolatier said from behind him.

The bishop turned to face him and found the chocolatier had changed. There was a deadly look on his face. "I have made a special treat for you," he said, holding out a little sealed golden bag of what must be chocolates. "Perhaps you could share them with the pope, as a little token of Ceres."

The tone of the chocolatier's voice was odd; the bishop could not pinpoint its meaning. Had these chocolates been poisoned? Was the chocolatier attempting a long-distance assassination? Or was there something else to this?

The bishop took the bag and thanked the chocolatier, who opened his eyes wide as he handed them over. There was a message in this gesture, but the bishop had no idea what it could be.

"Will you make me a promise?" the chocolatier asked.

"If you like. What promise are you looking for?"

"That you will not eat these chocolates until you have set foot on Earth, and when you do you will remember us here on Ceres."

"You have my word." The bishop smiled. But the whole conversation was too odd, and he quickly made his exit.

# (17.)

On the ship, the bishop sent out word for people to gather in the dining area.

His intention was to tell them that they were free to go, that after all their worries, Ceres had turned out to be a bit of an anti-climax, an inconvenience rather than a catastrophe. But it became clear in his first few interactions that this news had already gotten around.

More surprising was that the passengers had been told that the Frank Sinatra was impounded and would be held indefinitely. Passengers would have to book travel on other ships. There were, of course, no direct flights to Earth. Instead, they would have go back to Mars, or go to one station colony or another where Scoundrel Lines could arrange passage.

When the passengers had gathered as requested, the bishop explained that the entire episode had been an attempt to arrest one of the passengers: David Elsman. He said that David must have understood this and taken his own life rather than be taken by the Fascists.

"The Fuhrer did not give me any specifics, but it appears that he took Professor Elsman to be a spy. I have no idea whether or not that accusation is true. Dr. Elsman presented himself to me as a scholar, and that is what I took him to be."

Some of the passengers wanted the full details of the meeting with the Fuhrer, and the bishop did his best to answer all questions honestly. One young woman asked if the bishop felt that the Fuhrer was possessed of mesmerizing power, as was generally believed.

"No," the bishop answered, "but he is a very intelligent man, and he is convinced of his superiority. That gives him a certain, um, air."

The rest of the bishop's afternoon was spent in conversation with individual passengers or with little groups who wanted the bishop's advice on visiting New Nuremberg and on making travel arrangements.

The bishop advised that everyone spend at least some time seeing the city and meeting the locals. He had no reason to think this presented any danger to them, and the place was genuinely worth seeing.

During free moments he assessed his own travel options.

There were eleven ships leaving Ceres in the next week. Four of them were headed out toward the Jovian colonies. A little stirring of temptation erupted at the thought of just chucking it all and heading out into the wild.

But this was not a serious consideration. He was either going to Earth or to Mars, so he asked the Web to map out the fastest options.

There was a ship leaving in six days direct to Mars. It was a freighter, and not much of one, but it would have him home in his own bed in a little over seven weeks.

There was a passenger ship to Mars that was leaving in just a day. But it would make two station colony stops on the way, and get into Mars eighteen days after the freighter.

On the other hand, if the trip was to be to Earth, the options were far more extensive. There were dozens of station colonies, and scores of combinations of ships picking up and dropping off passengers. The Web could probably have put together thousands of itineraries if asked. But why ask?

The quickest trip left in two days on a freighter for an eighteen-day-trip to a station colony, where another ship would pick him up eight days later and make a forty-day trip to the moon. From the moon he could take a bus down to Earth.

There was a much more comfortable option to Earth on a passenger ship, but it did not leave for eleven days, and did not arrive in Earth orbit for nearly five months. In a way, this option was the most attractive. To stay in New Nuremberg for eleven days, making day trips or overnights to other Cerean cities, sounded like a vacation.

Five months in transit didn't sound like much fun, but at least the ship would have the comforts of passenger travel. He would be able to work, to read, and to visit with other passengers. He called the Asantes. This was the option that they had chosen. Five months of whist and conversation did not sound so bad.

But it felt like much too long to be away from his duties. He would likely not see Coolidge-town again for at least a full year. And he felt ready to head back to Mars right now: how would he feel when he had been away from home for months and months?

If he was to head back to Mars and just put off the Ad Limina, he decided the best course was to take the freighter, getting back home as quickly as he could, and planning another trip for a year or two down the road. He called the papal nuncio for the off-Earth missions and left a message detailing the options and giving his preference to return to his diocese and delay the trip to Rome.

The lag time was now about thirteen minutes, and the nuncio had already called expressing his concern for the bishop. When he got the bishop's message, the Nuncio—a punctilious man—would send a return message immediately. This left about a half hour for the bishop to pray the Angelus and to shower.

Drying off and readying himself for a second engagement with the Fuhrer, the bishop listened to the return call from the Nuncio. The message was brief, impersonal, and extremely clear. "Do not return to Mars. Proceed to Earth with all reasonable haste. Convey papal salutations to the leader of the Cerean government."

# (18.)

The leader of the Cerean government was sitting in a green armchair when the bishop was brought to him for the second time. Beside him were two men whose faces the bishop recognized instantly: Eugenio Sacco, the vice-Fuhrer, and Stephen Reston, the information minister.

The meeting was not in the Chancellery, but in Mr. Reston's home. Though the room was less imposing than the Fuhrer's office, it maintained the aesthetic of dark wood, empty spaces, and masculinity.

The windows along one wall were large rectangles. In front of them was a great wooden desk. The Fuhrer and the other men were sitting at an imposing fireplace between two large built-in cabinets with tall rectangular wood and glass doors.

On a carpet in front of the fireplace were two armchairs and a sofa arranged around a sturdy wooden coffee table.

The three men stood when the bishop entered the room and offered him the victory salute. He did not return it, but, doing his best to be tactful, he thanked the Fuhrer for the invitation.

The Fuhrer introduced Sacco and then Reston. Both shook the bishop's hand vigorously. The Fuhrer sat and Reston motioned for the bishop to take a seat on the couch next to Sacco. Reston then moved toward a small bar near the windows.

"What can I get you to drink?" he asked the bishop in an accent that the bishop thought was New York or New Jersey. But it could just as well have been Scotland. The bishop was not good with Earth's many accents.

"Whatever you gentlemen are drinking, please," the bishop answered, noting that each had a tankard of what might be beer.

"You are a beer drinker?" Reston asked in a friendly tone.

"Not a well-educated one, but an appreciative one," the bishop answered. "I mostly drink simple Martian pilsners or ales."

"Simple is often a very good quality in beer," Sacco said.

"But this one you will find a little more complex, perhaps," Reston said as he handed a tankard to the bishop. "It is a very old variety, made by Bavarian Catholic monks since the late Middle Ages, I am told."

The beer was more pungent than the bishop was used to, but he assured his host that it was delightful. "Is the choice of Catholic beer in my honor?"

Reston laughed, "I should probably just say yes, but I drink this several nights a week."

The Fuhrer seemed content to let Reston act as host—a role at which he excelled. The Fuhrer participated with a small comment here or there, letting the other men talk pleasantly for a long while before getting to business.

When the moment seemed right, the bishop told the Fuhrer that he had been instructed to convey the pope's salutations to him personally.

The Fuhrer thanked the bishop and said, "Some of your prelates, though I am not certain where his holiness stands, have made very encouraging public remarks. I have the sense that a good part of the hierarchy understands the moment of crisis we face, how humanity is at risk of squandering its entire heritage and becoming simply reprobate."

"Well, I am not instructed to convey any other message from the Holy Father, but it is certainly true that the Church is deeply concerned about the current state of humanity."

The bishop was not comfortable speaking like a diplomat. He knew there were ways of saying things without saying them and withholding things that seemed entirely out in the open. But he did not know how that game was played.

For a while, the Fuhrer seemed to be gently interrogating him, seeking information on the internal state of the Church and on the general disposition of the bishops on several fronts. The bishop answered honestly, in most cases, that he was quite isolated from the internal workings of the Church in his role as Bishop of Mars.

"But you are on your way to see the pope," the Fuhrer offered.

"Yes. I have been a bishop for nine years, and I have never been to Rome. The pope has called me to make the visit I should technically have made years ago."

"An *Ad Limina*," the Fuhrer said. "It has been explained to me, and it seems like a great deal of effort just to overcome a few minutes of delay in a video conference."

"We believe that physical touch is essential for some things."

"Yes, I suppose," the Fuhrer said, but he did not say what he supposed. Instead, he told the bishop that his own Latin was poor, but even he could make out that *Ad Limina* meant something in the neighborhood of "to the light." He then gave a little speech about how

- 71 -

humanity had better begin its own pilgrimage to the light soon—before a darkness deeper than the one that had descended after the fall of the Roman Empire came down upon everyone.

The bishop did not interrupt the speech, despite its obvious flaw. He supposed that some things must just be borne. And toward the end of the speech, the Fuhrer got to the point.

"The Catholic Church is, like all of humanity, in a dangerous place at the moment. I believe that the Church still has a great deal to offer humanity, and I would like the pope to know that good relations with us are still possible, and they will bear great fruit in the coming decades."

With that, the Fuhrer simply looked the bishop hard in the eye. His face was relaxed, as if the beer had been double potent. The bishop was considering his reply when the Fuhrer's face seemed suddenly to change. Or, rather, the bishop's understanding of it suddenly changed.

The Fuhrer was not awaiting a reply; he was glaring. This was not diplomatic talk; it was a threat.

And the implications of the threat were enormous. To make such a threat was to admit that war was coming and that the Church could choose to ally itself with the Fascists and survive, or defy them and die.

The bishop had heard the Fuhrer described as a gangster, and the description had seemed inapt. Politicians are not gangsters.

But at this moment, the man looking at him could be described in no other way. The green cushions, the clean and bright windows, the beer, and the conversation were all trappings. The reality skulked in the ice-blue eyes that glared at him: brute, remorseless violence.

# (19.)

The bishop found it hard to sleep on the freighter. The air in his cramped quarters was stale, and the spin of the small ship offered only about half the gravity of Mars.

Nor did the common areas provide much comfort.

There was a mess hall with a sticky, gray, no-slip floor that seemed never to be quite dry. The seating was four to a table, with both seats and tables made cheaply and bolted firmly to the floor. The furniture was as gray as the floor, and only slightly less sticky.

The cook was good, however, and the meals were fine, if plain. The crew of five seemed only slightly resentful of the fourteen passengers they had to take on as a "humanism gesture," as one of them put it.

The bishop found two Catholics aboard—one crew member and one passenger from the Frank Sinatra. He celebrated daily Mass with them, adjusting the timing to suit the crewman's work schedule. The crewman seemed pleased to attend each day, but refused communion. They used a little office most days, but there was also a common room they could use if no one else was present.

It was one of two common rooms on the freighter, which the passengers referred to as "the big room" and "the little room."

The big room had a pay-per-use media lounge for which the passengers and crew created a schedule. Each person was scheduled for one hour per day. The rest of each day was first-come, first-served. The bishop gave his hour each day to one of the crew and made do with the basic media in his cabin. There he spent at least two hours each day writing for pleasure, a couple more reading, and a few more communicating with his priests and staff on Mars, either by letter or by holo message.

He also granted several interviews to media personalities who wanted the inside story of the seizing of the Frank Sinatra. The story of the hijacked ship had become a sensation, and the bishop had the special distinction of having met twice with the Fuhrer.

At first the interviewers were not certain what to do with the bishop, given he had been in their spotlight so recently as a villain and now they wanted to make him a hero.

The general narrative they settled on was of a bishop who had once challenged the UNAC but now, in the face of adversity, was cooperating with the Fleet.

The bishop could not help but laugh.

Less funny, however, was the news that several Fleet warships had been dispatched to high orbit above Ceres. Talk of war proliferated, and with it a communal alertness that bordered on giddy.

The passengers gathered in the mess hall each evening, the bishop among them, as the news channels discussed the rising tensions, the various developments.

"Tonight, there is talk of a full invasion of Ceres if the unregistered ship Frank Sinatra is not surrendered," the announcer intoned gravely.

The scene switched to a military spokesman.

"Hadamar is playing a dangerous game," the spokesman said. "Fleet policy is to enforce the Law of

Free Transit. It may be that he thinks we will not commit resources in defense of an unregistered ship. If that is the case, the self-styled Fuhrer is making a grave mistake."

The attempt to dismiss the Fuhrer with a phrase like "self-styled" struck the bishop as a sign of weakness. He was the leader of millions, whether the Fleet liked it or not. And the bishop could hardly imagine euphemisms such as "commit resources" striking fear into the hearts of the Fascists.

"Despite these clear warnings from the Fleet," the announcer went on, "The Fuhrer remains defiant.

"In a speech delivered at the New Nuremberg Chancellery, he asserted that Ceres is ready to confront any invasion that might come."

The scene now switched to the vast square in front of the Chancellery. The square looked nothing like it had on the day the bishop crossed it on foot and alone.

It was jammed now with tens of thousands of cheering people, all with faces turned up ecstatically to the balcony from which the Fuhrer spoke.

"We have the right to defend ourselves. It is the most ancient right of nations. Without it the very concept of freedom is meaningless. We will arrest spies wherever they might be hiding and by whatever means are required. If they hide amidst tourists on a transport ship, then we will do what we have done.

"If we are not given room to breathe, we will make room for ourselves and for our children."

The roar of the crowd was deafening, and then the scene switched again, this time to a UNAC lawyer.

"The Fuhrer is claiming that he can seize shipping, but there is no legal basis for such seizures. He has no legal authority to interfere with shipping. This is the most basic law of the solar system."

Now the scene returned to the Fuhrer shouting angrily from the Chancellery balcony.

"I remind the arrogant bureaucrats of the UNAC that there are millions of New Fascists spread out across the solar system in station colonies, on Jovian moon colonies, and even on Earth. Ceres has a duty to protect them and their interests."

Now back to the lawyer.

"This is another new idea from the Fuhrer. He seems to be claiming the right to defend his allies even if it means doing so within UNAC states. It is not at all clear how he means this, but it certainly has warlike implications."

Now to a politician from the General Assembly.

"The Fuhrer is looking for a pretext for war, and too many of us are not taking him seriously. We are not prepared to face this threat either materially or psychologically. We must prepare for war."

Now to another politician from the General Assembly.

"Well, I have to say there is just too much irresponsible talk of war from some members of this body. The core value we are all sworn to uphold is tolerance. But people seem to have forgotten that. Tolerance is a difficult thing. It applies even to the Fascists. There will always be such movements, but people want to live in a free and tolerant society. If we let things take their course, this movement will fade, people will come to their senses. Given a choice between a free and tolerant society and an aggressive, oppressive society, I think we can trust in the long run that people will do the right thing, so long as we do not let warmongering lead us to something tragic and unnecessary."

Now back to the news reader.

"International Criminal Court warrants have been issued for several figures thought to have been key to the seizing the Frank Sinatra, though no warrants have yet been issued for the Fuhrer or any of the High Command. No arrests are expected, but for those who have had warrants issued against them, travel will now be severely limited."

"Why not just send them a strongly worded letter," one of the passengers sitting near the bishop offered sarcastically. "It would mean about as much to them."

The bishop was tempted to chime in with his agreement. The cold violence he had seen in the Fuhrer's face when last they met had not faded from his memory.

He imagined the Fuhrer watching all this bluster and talk of the Law of Free Transit and being entirely unimpressed. That meant that the only party impressed by the UNAC's displays was the UNAC itself: a dangerous reality, one that might convince the UNAC that it was confronting threats when, in fact, it was encouraging them.

The bishop recalled one of Saint Letisha's aphorisms, "The proud believe an untruth, and so are in danger."

# (20.)

The bishop thought it would be unseemly to share these thoughts with others. His role – the role he had willingly given himself to – was priestly. He tried to avoid the temptation to get publicly involved in politics because to be a priest, and especially a bishop, meant remaining as free as possible to minister to all who came. Giving an impression of political fervor would guarantee that some would be driven away from pastoral care, even when in need.

Feeling he might not be able to remain detached, however, the bishop no longer joined the other passengers each night for the ad hoc news hour and political discussion. He occupied himself, instead, with study of the station colony toward which the freighter was headed.

It was an older model—not one of the gigantic stations they had been building the last few years. Its population was a mere 568, and like many station colonies, it was not just a place to live and work, but was a community with a particular mission.

The Melton Post-Humanity Research Foundation had bought the station nearly a decade ago from a company that went bankrupt trying to build and lease station space to universities. The sums to buy a complete station were enormous, so the Melton people sold their Earth properties and their various labs around the solar system to make this one, grand purchase.

Moving all of their operations to the new MPH Research Station allowed them to concentrate their efforts in one place and to conduct research without interference from governments, an important precaution, given the legal and moral questions raised by the foundation's mission.

The bishop first became aware of the problematic nature of the station's work on the sixth or seventh day out from Ceres, when one of his two parishioners on the ship, the lone Catholic crewmember, came to confession.

The crewman, Eddie Cho, had to bring in a chair from his own quarters because there was only one in the bishop's tiny cabin. The two men sat face to face with hardly enough room to keep their knees from bumping.

The bishop folded his hands, leaned forward, and bowed his head as Eddie spoke.

Eddie blessed himself and paused just long enough to inhale deeply before pouring out his concerns. Primarily, this came down to a growing fear that he was involved in "material cooperation with evil."

"You see, bishop, we are carrying supplies to our next stop that will be used in immoral experiments. People always talk about how the Jovian colonies are lawless, but there is no law in any of the colonies, really.

"What goes on in some of these places is bad— and I'm not talking about the brothels or the nano-V or any of that stuff that people usually talk about."

The bishop looked up, "Bad how, Eddie?" he asked without intonation. "I am afraid I am not really sure what you are referring to."

The bishop imagined that every generation since people first took to the seas has probably had its share of men like Eddie: men who did not mind the long stretches away from land and who took the trade of the voyager seriously. They took pride in being what used to be called an "able seaman"—able to take care of themselves and their ships.

But now tears were streaming down Eddie's face as he tried to find the words to make a good confession. "It is probably a sin to say it," he said, fighting to speak calmly over his own emotions, "but I like the Fascists better than I like these people. At least with the Fascists, it is all above board. They wouldn't do these things."

The bishop sat quietly and waited for Eddie to name whatever was so upsetting him. He considered for a moment that Eddie might just be overwrought. It was always possible that the crewman was having an exaggerated reaction to something that was not so bad after all.

"They kill people where we are going," Eddie said finally, "and I think I am helping them to do it."

The bishop was taken aback for a moment.

"Eddie, how do they kill people?"

"I am not sure what they do, we are never in port more than a day or two, but other crew that I have served with have talked about how they grow clones to experiment on, and..."

Eddie really didn't know much, but what he knew was enough to convince the bishop that Eddie was indeed committing "material cooperation with evil."

The bishop asked Eddie whether he was willing to give up his work on the freighter and find another way to make a living. He was surprised to find how readily Eddie said yes. Apparently, his anguish over parts of his job had been growing for months, and he had become ready to do whatever was necessary to set things right.

Eddie had a few more sins to confess, and the bishop listened patiently before laying his hands on Eddie's head and pronouncing absolution.

"Should I quit now?" Eddie asked.

"No, I don't think so. I think you have a duty to see the ship safely into port before that. There are the passengers and your fellow crew to consider. But once in port, let's see about booking you passage home."

"I have a sister on Earth," Eddie said. "She lives in a city called Seoul, have you heard of it?"

"I think I have. Is it an American city?"

Eddie laughed. "Nobody ever knows where Seoul is," he said.

"I am terrible with Earth cities," the bishop admitted with a shrug.

"We are a long way from Earth," Eddie offered.

"I suppose so," the bishop said. "Is your sister your only family?"

"My parents are both gone," Eddie said. "To tell you the truth, I am not really sure where to go. My sister and brother-in-law have five small children. I don't think this is the best moment to ask her to take me in."

"We have about two weeks to think about that before we make port," the bishop assured him, and— despite the uncertainty—Eddie seemed genuinely at peace as he left.

From that time on, the bishop spent time each day finding out all he could about the Melton Foundation.

Much of what he found was morally unproblematic, even noble. The foundation had been among the first organizations to create substitute organs to cure diseases. Their great initial success had been in making syntho-pancreatic organs for those with diabetes. They had played a major role in developing, and now held several important and lucrative patents for, neuron regenerators to overcome paralysis.

But their philosophy was free-wheeling. They believed that neither religion nor government should impede pure science—which they called "the way to human progress." They were generous in their mission statement in admitting that every person should be free to live by his or her own moral code, adding a quote from someone named Casey to the effect that: "At the heart of liberty is the right to define one's own concept of existence, of meaning, of the universe, and of the mystery of human life." This philosophy allowed them to say that they respected all religions and all moralities while being bound by none of them.

They were adamant that there was nothing particularly sacred about human biology. To limit science in its study and development of humanity, they said, was a great injustice.

As far as the bishop could tell, this meant that they felt free to do whatever they wanted to particular human beings so long as it expanded the horizons and improved the well-being of humanity in total.

"The Melton Foundation for Post Human Studies exists to expand human horizons, and—where possible—to move beyond them to new horizons as new beings with formerly un-imagined powers and unlimited life spans," their mission statement concluded.

Reaching for his beads, the bishop said sardonically to himself, "See, I am making all things new."

Mass each day remained an intimate affair, though the bishop's congregation doubled one morning when a new couple, Meg and Bill Hemmer from Lincoln, Nebraska, showed up. They were non-denominational Christians and had shared a dinner table with the bishop the evening before. After a long and friendly conversation about the Gospel of John, the bishop had invited them to attend.

They participated very little, but told the bishop they appreciated having fellow Christians to pray with. They suggested that a Bible study might be a nice way to share time together for the remainder of the trip, to which the bishop heartily agreed.

The Hemmers were natural recruiters, and the nightly Bible study they arranged had nine members by the time the trip came near its conclusion.

Eddie Cho managed to make the study most nights, and the bishop grew more and more impressed with him. When Eddie attended, the entire group seemed calmer and more deeply in tune with the readings. His comments always seemed to get to the point without any showiness, though the points Eddie got from the readings were almost always surprising.

Once, when the group was discussing the ninth chapter of Mark's Gospel, everyone seemed to agree that Jesus was speaking figuratively when he said, "If your eye causes you to sin, pluck it out."

"We have to be careful not to take these things too literally," one older woman said maternally.

"I think our problem is that we don't take this line literally enough," Eddie replied.

When he said such things there was no hint of controversy in his tone. He simply said what he thought, and seemed to expect others to do so as well.

The bishop, though appreciating Eddie's vigor for the Gospel, was concerned this time that Eddie might be missing the subtlety of the text.

"Do you think that Jesus would want you to cut your eye out?" the older woman asked Eddie.

"No," Eddie said. "That's what I mean. If we take this literally, we will not cut out our eye."

Now the bishop suspected Eddie was confused about the meaning of the word "literally." He was about to wade into the discussion when Eddie explained himself.

"The word we forget to take literally is 'if,'" Eddie said. "Jesus said 'if your eye causes you to sin,' but, speaking literally, your eye cannot cause you to sin, and neither can your hand or any other part of your body. Only your will can cause you to sin. If some part of your will wants to sin, you have to be firm with yourself and cut it out."

The bishop smiled.

Such moments were common with Eddie.

As the ship's plasma engines came to life again, slowing the freighter for docking with the Melton Station, the bishop grew increasingly uneasy. He supposed he must be the first Catholic bishop to set foot in this place. He wondered about the reception he would get, and about his own reaction to the people who lived and worked here.

Strange twists had led to this visit, however, and he took some comfort in this fact. Coming here had been almost completely out of his control, but that did not mean it was accidental.

# (21.)

The reception on the Melton Station could not have been less like the one on Ceres. The freighter docked and several agents from shipping and receiving floated aboard. They informed the passengers that they were free to go wherever they liked on the station, and then got to work checking manifests and arranging to offload cargo.

Mrs. Hemmer was the only passenger who had the sense to ask about accommodations before the last of the agents disappeared into the holds. "There are guest rooms available and several dining options," she was told. "See the holo assistant in the terminal."

The passengers hung together as they made their way to the terminal. There, the hologram was helpful and polite and, apparently, a joke. It was essentially a cartoon character in 3D. It was programmed to offer all of the assistance one would expect from a hospitality hologram, but it was a walking talking fence-post, wearing a T-shirt with the word "HUMAN" across its chest.

At first the bishop just took it to be an odd affectation, a bit of silliness of the kind that appealed to the playful minds of scientists. But, again, Mrs. Hemmer was on top of things before anyone else.

"It is funny, in a way," she said sheepishly, "if it were not about something so serious." None of the other passengers knew what she was talking about.

"It's a post," she said expectantly, as if she were making the thing obvious.

Still, no one got it until Mr. Hemmer groaned, "Oh, that's not good. It's a 'post-human,' get it?"

The bishop was surprised to find how deeply offended he felt at the joke. He thought he had learned just to roll with the flippancies of the "Age of Expansion," as people sometimes called this bizarre era.

"What trivializing mockery," he thought. He realized at that moment how little he wanted to spend eight days here, how badly he wanted just to be on his way.

But once inside the station, his disposition changed almost immediately. It was another cylinder—in fact a genuine O'Neill Cylinder—much smaller than the cylindrical city of New Nuremberg, but in its own way just as striking. The interior of the spinning barrel was divided into six strips that ran down its length. Three of the strips were inhabited, and the other three were windows that let bona fide sunshine in, apparently through some clever use of mirrors.

The bishop was not at all sure how the windows worked or what technical magic was performed to protect the population from deadly radiation. All he knew at that moment was the effect of the place, and it was stunning.

It could not have been more than a kilometer from one end of the station to the other. But the population was so much smaller than that of New Nuremberg that the interior was mostly parkland.

Hyper-modern homes were set at leisurely distances from one another along little streams or at the crest of grassy hills. Several campuses of larger buildings, probably the labs, clustered here and there.

The "post-human" had directed the passengers to the Red Barn, where they could arrange rooms if they liked or shop or get something to eat. And there it was, on a hill surrounded by bike trails and grass and shrubbery. It stood out because of its size and color, and all paths seemed to lead toward it.

It was, indeed, a barn, but rendered in a hyper-modernist mode. The bishop liked the look of it. Very little of the architecture on Mars could be called whimsical, and this barn was.

The elevators to the "floor" of the station were less impressive than those at New Nuremberg, but the greeter at the bottom was very impressive.

As the doors of the elevator slid open, the passengers came face to face with a male lion. He had a massive mane and eyes that were either terribly sad or lazily malignant—the bishop could not tell which.

"Don't worry about him," a young woman nearby called out. "He is incapable of aggression."

In spite of her assurance, the passengers remained immobile in the elevator.

"Sailor, come," the young woman called out, and the beast padded its way to her.

"We greet newcomers," the woman said. "I am Kendra and this is Sailor. He's one of five GM lions that roam free in Area 1, which you are now in. Quite a few other animals also roam free here, but none will hurt you. They are genetically modified to make aggression impossible. They will not even defend themselves should someone hurt them."

A few of the passengers stepped toward Sailor to run their hands through his mane. Most, however, including the bishop, seemed just as happy to keep distance between themselves and the lion.

As they walked to the barn, they passed another lion asleep near the path, and some kangaroos, a few dogs, and lots of sheep. The bishop wondered if the little lambs that romped on their new legs ever lay down with the lions.

With genetic modification, anything seemed possible.

As they neared the Barn, they were able to take its measure. It seemed to be about three or four stories tall and maybe a hundred meters long.

The interior was an odd space, with lofts and stalls that housed various shops and eateries. Each of these maintained a whimsical take on the barn theme. One could rent rooms here, and the passengers did, not wanting to return to the staleness of the freighter's accommodations.

The bishop's room was on the second floor. He would have settled for anything after the dankness of his freighter quarters, but this was elegant and comfortable. Beyond a wide and inviting bed, a desk, and an overstuffed chair, he had a window overlooking parkland and animals all bathed in real sunlight.

The bishop stood for a long time taking in the Melton Station. He had just decided to lie down when a knock sounded on his door.

Eddie Cho.

"Please come in, Eddie," the bishop said gladly.

"Or perhaps you can come out and treat me to dinner," Eddie answered.

The bishop wasn't sure what to make of this, but went along. "Sure, just a minute. Let me put on my shoes."

"You're not going to ask why you are buying me dinner?"

"Well, I..."

"I am celebrating my retirement from freighter service, and I thought you would want to celebrate with me."

Tears welled up in Eddie's eyes as he said it. The bishop supposed it was in part because Eddie really was happy to have done the right thing, and in part because he was leaving work that he genuinely loved.

"No sacrifice for the love of goodness goes unrewarded, Eddie. You are on a new adventure now."

"I know I am," Eddie said, wiping his eyes and smiling. "That's why you're buying."

# (22.)

The bishop left the curtains open when he went to sleep, and he awoke, as he had hoped, to the light of the sun.

For the eight days he was to be in port, he had little to do but share meals with Eddie and the Hemmers, chat with any locals who were willing, and stroll.

He found himself taking intense pleasure in his strolls around the green paths of the Melton Station.

The station designers had created a brilliant illusion of open space, placing hills and knolls, trees, wooden fences, and even rustic tunnels along the path to give it a rolling farm-country feel and to induce the walker into a sense of passing along miles of natural meandering trail.

What most impressed the bishop, however, was the sunlight. It did not come from Samsung or Windotec or any other image maker. In fact, he could see the sun itself, reflected in the mirrors. He could hardly get over the fact that day after day he was bathing in real—if reflected—sunshine.

Even in the greenhouses of Mars, the sun was not like this. It was smaller and almost always red from the dust in the atmosphere.

The animals of the Melton Station engendered less cheerfulness in the bishop. Their genetically pacified temperaments were supposed to take the menace out of them, but it did not, entirely. They remained formidable creatures, and when he was out in the open with them, the bishop found they still possessed some quality that both drew him and frightened him

He was particularly drawn to a herd of animals called wildebeests. Their physicality was intoxicating. He walked among them as if among angels, cautiously and in awe.

He enjoyed their capriciousness, the way the whole herd would disappear and the way they would suddenly reappear where he did not expect them. This gave the sight of them the feeling of a blessing.

He looked for them as he walked the paths, and when he found them, he watched as if they held a secret. They did, indeed, seem to hold a secret—something wonderful that simply refused to be named.

It was on the second afternoon, as he was among the wildebeests, just walking with them and patting their high shoulders, that the bishop looked up to see an animal that was truly unexpected. In fact, at first sight, the bishop thought it must be an escapee from one of the science labs. The creature was a chimpanzee, he was fairly sure at the time, though later he learned that the more precise word for him was bonobo.

The bishop had seen great apes on Mars, and had been fascinated by them. But nothing could compare to coming upon one sitting at the crest of a little hill just a few yards away. Most unnerving of all was the fact that the ape seemed to be studying the bishop intently, and he was wearing coveralls.

How like a human this creature was. Or, perhaps, how like a bonobo humanity is. Either way, there was something terrifying in the similarity. What might such a creature be thinking? What might he do?

For a moment the bishop considered simply remaining among the wildebeests and passing by. Perhaps, if it was an escapee, the ape could get violent.

But something in the expression of the creature stopped the bishop. The wildebeests continued on their loping way until the bishop found himself standing alone before the staring bonobo.

The strangeness of what happened next was like the lighting of a fuse.

In the months and years that lay ahead, that fuse would set off a series of explosions in the very soul of the man who now stood at the foot of the little hill.

The bonobo wrote with his right index finger in the air. This, of course, the bishop had seen done thousands of times by humans. Implanted computing and 3D projection were practically ancient technologies. Someone here on the Melton station had simply installed a comcom in the bonobo.

The letters hung in the air as the creature wrote.

"Do not be scared," they said. "I can speak."

"You can speak?" the bishop asked, wondering if the animal had been trained to do this trick, and wondering whether some group of station dwellers was now hanging back, watching as the joke played out.

"I can speak," the bonobo said in a gravelly voice. He did not move.

The bishop was dumbfounded. He looked around to see who might be responsible for this extraordinary little show.

"It is no trick," the bonobo said, noticing the bishop's consternation. "My name is Doug."

As he said this, the bonobo rose on his legs, leaned forward on the knuckles of his left hand, and extended his right to the bishop.

"Pleased to meet you, Doug," the bishop said, shaking the long hand.

"I wrote in the air to warn you because some people are nearly frightened out of their skins when I first speak."

"Thank you," the bishop answered. His mouth was dry. "Very considerate."

"I am not an ape," Doug told him as he sat back down at the crest of the little hill. "I am probably as human as you are."

"I see," the bishop said in a moment of flustered dishonesty.

Doug went on, "I am the result of an experiment. This station is dedicated to practical research, but it also does a great deal of pure science. I am the result of pure science, so to speak."

"I see," the bishop said again, unable to formulate any more of a response.

"A team decided to see if a human brain could be induced to live within an ape. You would be surprised at how many applications there now are for this kind of research. I was created almost three decades ago, and I am still the subject of frequent studies."

The elocution that Doug had just given seemed to establish that no trick was afoot, though that possibility could not entirely be ruled out. The whole situation left the bishop uncertain.

Doug filled the silence. "You are a Catholic something or other, I am told."

"Yes, indeed. I am a something or other," the bishop answered wryly. "But the official title is bishop."

"I am interested in Catholicism," Doug told him. "The study of religions is a hobby of mine."

"Are you a religious person?" the bishop asked.

Doug stared for a moment.

"Thank you, bishop, for referring to me as a person. Some people take a long time to see past appearances."

"Yes, Doug, of course," the bishop said.

"I do not know how religious I am," Doug said. "I didn't really know anything about God until a few years ago when a preacher came through here. We spoke several times, and he got me thinking about things I had never bothered with before. Now I believe in God, and lately I have been thinking that the Jews have the most convincing ideas about God."

"Indeed they do," the bishop said. "Catholics believe that the Jews are God's chosen people."

"I have always been unclear on that point," Doug said, leaning back on his long arms. "Would you mind sitting down and talking for a while?"

"Not at all," the bishop said with genuine delight. Everything was simple now. Doug wanted to hear about God. That, as it turned out, was the bishop's specialty.

He sat upon the hill, and the two of them talked until the mirrored sun grew dim. Then they went to a little French restaurant in the Red Barn for dinner, where they were joined by Eddie Cho.

The bishop made a fairly stumbling introduction in which he tried to explain Doug, more or less tripping over his words until Eddie simply held out his hand and said, "Pleased to meet you, Doug."

Since leaving the freighter, Eddie seemed to greet everything with serenity. The bishop began to think that he knew a place where Eddie would fit in.

Over dinner, Eddie explained to Doug why he had quit the freighter and that he was now considering his next steps. Doug was surprised at the moral objections to the Melton Station's work, but took them quite seriously.

"People talk a great deal about ethics here," Doug explained to Eddie, "But I have never heard anyone talk about good and evil the way you do."

Eddie explained, occasionally with help from the bishop, why Catholics believed every single human life had an immeasurable dignity. This was an idea that appealed to Doug immediately. He felt that this was one of the things that had attracted him to the Jews. Eddie explained that the way the Melton Foundation raised cloned human offspring in artificial wombs and conducted experiments on them to try out ideas about post-humanity violated the Catholic belief in human dignity.

"If there is no God, then there is no special dignity to these little clones," Doug observed. "If there is no God, then there is not much to them. They are just little animals. They have no thoughts or feelings to worry about. Why not experiment on them for the good of humanity?"

Neither Eddie nor the bishop was sure what to make of this pronouncement until Doug spoke again.

He smiled and said, "But, as I told Mark earlier, I believe there is a God."

"Right," Eddie said. "There is a God."

"And I have been wondering what he thinks about me," Doug said.

"You are his child," Eddie said.

The bishop envied and admired the simplicity with which Eddie said it. He knew that as a bishop he should be more like that.

Doug pursed his lips in a very bonobo-like manner. "I suspected as much," he said with a broad bonobo smile. They all laughed.

Doug quickly grew serious again, however, and looked at the bishop almost imploringly.

"Am I a child of God?" he asked. "I was created as an experiment. Doesn't that make me something less than a child of God?"

The bishop furrowed his brow and studied Doug's face.

"I don't know how much of Earth's history you will remember, but the Church faced a similar question when it first came into contact with the indigenous people of the Americas.

"Slave traders argued that the Indians were not people because they often wore little clothing and they were relatively small and brown, and a host of other things.

"A bishop named De las Casas argued that they were, in fact, human and they, therefore, had rights. This argument is one of the first arguments ever made for universal human rights."

"I had not heard that, but bishop—"

"I know, Doug, that is not exactly the same thing, but it establishes the principle—all human beings have the same rights, no matter their appearance or condition of life."

"But bishop, you are avoiding the key question— am I human? I believe I am; I am certainly sentient in a human way, does that—"

"We Catholics are very careful to avoid talk of sentience as a condition for humanity. One is not more human because one is more intelligent, nor less human because one is less intelligent. There are some people whose level of intelligence might be lower than that of an animal. So what? One is human, and a child of God, because one is a member of the human species, the crown of God's creation."

Doug seemed more exasperated than satisfied with this answer.

"Bishop, I ... I ... you have not understood my question..."

"Doug isn't sure what species he is," Eddie interrupted. He did not look at the bishop as he said it, but kept his gaze steadily on Doug. He smiled.

Doug did not smile but looked quizzically at Eddie.

"I think the problem might be with the word 'created,'" Eddie said. "You said you were created as an experiment. I don't think so."

"Ah, right," the bishop said. "You were not 'created' out of nothing. You began as a clone, or maybe by artificial insemination, just like most people these days."

"And anyway," Eddie added, "Creation is a matter of both body and soul. Even a clone is created by God, in the sense that everything that goes into making the clone is God's work, and the soul is directly made by God. In your case, once you existed, they took away most of your body and put what was left into a bonobo. Isn't that right?"

"Yes, I suppose. I was still prenatal when they did it, but essentially, yes."

"But they did not take away all of your body, and they did not take away any of your soul."

"Yes. Right," the bishop said.

"God made you," Eddie said, returning to eating. "You are one of His children."

Tears formed in Doug's eyes. He stared down into the tablecloth.

"I have thought of myself as a human. But since I have been thinking about God, I have felt unsure about ... about whether I was human in a ... religious way. Does that make sense?"

"Yes," the bishop said, patting Doug's shoulder. "What doesn't make sense is what was done to you. It certainly makes sense that it would raise every kind of question."

"Do you agree with Eddie? Am I a child of God?" Doug asked, and his voice cracked as the words came out.

"Yes, Doug, I do. It is clear what you are."

# (23.)

The next morning, the bishop awoke with a headache. He had enjoyed his time with Doug and Eddie, but he had awakened in the night thinking about Doug as a child with no mother or father, raised as an experiment by people who just wanted to see what it would be like to put a human brain into an ape.

Now his jaw hurt from grinding his teeth as he slept. He told the unit to make his coffee black this morning, and he prayed his hours blankly, as if in a trance.

The bishop found himself wondering about Doug's love life. The thought of him with female bonobos was disgusting. But the thought of Doug in love with a human woman was equally upsetting. Had the people who made Doug not even considered this? Had it not occurred to them how cruel it was, what they had done?

But the real root of his foul mood did not occur to the bishop until he got into the shower. As he let the warm water massage his face, he said out loud, as if Jesus were standing by the sink listening, "I know he is going to ask. But if I baptize him it could be automatic excommunication. They will say I baptized an animal."

The man by the sink remained quiet.

"What I should do is ask the Vatican for permission to baptize him."

The bishop scrubbed his hair.

"But I don't want to ask permission. For one thing, they will take forever. The Church always takes forever on these things, and, actually, now that I think about it, the main thing is I feel like a creep even for asking permission. Why should I ask? Doug is a man. I feel like I would be insulting him if I asked."

He rinsed his hair.

"I don't know how they think about these things at the Vatican. I have never even been to the Vatican. What will they make of the bishop who baptized a chimpanzee?"

The bishop went on in that vein for a while, sometimes scolding, sometimes imploring the man by the sink. And then he just stood quietly under the running water, thinking of Doug.

"Why should I care what anyone says? He is a man," the bishop said out loud to the water pouring over him, and he poured out his tears to it in sadness for Doug, in joy for clarity, in horror for the world.

# (24.)

The bishop was right. Doug asked to be baptized.

He and Eddie met the bishop for a late breakfast and explained that Doug had come to the decision shortly after the bishop had gone to bed.

The bishop hugged Doug and then put his hands on Doug's cheeks. He kissed Doug's forehead. "God bless you, my brother," he said. "There is much rejoicing in Heaven today."

Over breakfast, the bishop questioned Doug about his decision, making sure that it had been made freely and that Doug genuinely knew what he was doing.

Doug's answers were simple and convincing. He explained that this had not just happened overnight. In fact, he felt that for the last few years God had been preparing him for the day when the bishop and Eddie would show up.

"That is how it usually happens," the bishop said. "We begin to feel we are being prepared for something, and then the Gospel finds its way in."

"And I am dying," Doug said.

At this, both Eddie and the bishop put down their silverware and rested their hands on the table.

"I am so sorry," the bishop said.

"I have developed tumors of the spine that no one can quite explain," Doug told them. "They seem to be simian in origin, but my spine is a fusion of simian and human tissues. The whole thing is a mess."

"How long have you known?"

"Several months," Doug said.

"Do you have a prognosis?" Eddie asked.

"It is likely that I will lose motor functions before long. They think I might go blind. There is no clear answer on how long I have to live. The range they give me at every check-up is between six months and a year or two."

They spent some time talking about life and death, and making preliminary plans for Doug's baptism.

After breakfast the three companions walked among the rolling hills of the Melton Station.

"Do you want to know something that really bothers me about dying?" Doug asked.

They nodded.

"I have a job. I make money, and I have never had anything to spend it on. I suppose they gave me the job working in the lab so that I would have some meaning in my life. And I like it well enough.

"But the money just builds up in my savings account. I always thought I would think of something to spend it on, that I was saving up for something. But it was all pointless. I wasn't saving up for anything. My whole life was just busy work, and I..."

As Doug was speaking, the Hemmers came around a rocky bend in the path. Doug stopped mid-sentence and stood silently. The Hemmers were wide-eyed.

"Doug can talk," Eddie said. "He's a man, but the scientists here experimented on him."

The Hemmers seemed to struggle inwardly for a moment with this odd, but somehow dispositive explanation. No one said anything, and the Hemmers seemed by increments to gain control of whatever revulsion they felt. In any case, they turned to their manners, of which they had a full supply.

"It is a pleasure to meet you," Mrs. Hemmer said, extending her hand. Mr. Hemmer followed suit.

As Doug began telling them how he had met the bishop and then Eddie, the Hemmers began really to relax. Conversation acted as a solvent, breaking down discomfort, and in a short while the back and forth was as easy as any on the porch back home.

Seemingly out of the blue, Doug asked if they would all like to see a trick, and before they could answer he took off running on his arms and legs at a speed that startled them. As he crested a hill he leapt into the air. He disappeared behind the crest and then came rocketing back into view on the back of a wildebeest.

The animal ran wildly, obviously spooked by Doug, but quickly recovered her composure and slowed to a trot. Using some imperceptible technique, Doug directed the enormous animal back toward his friends and trotted by laughing.

"We do this all the time," he shouted. "Bessy and I are old pals."

He crested another hill, turned Bessy again, and then got her to accelerate to a frightening speed across a flat, open area.

The sight of Doug riding was at once so outrageous and so graceful that the onlookers could hardly contain their laughter. Doug whistled and saluted and performed every kind of silliness, never seeming at all in danger of falling. And after a few minutes he circled back around, leapt off in front of his audience, landed on his feet, and took a grand bow to shouts and applause.

"You are full of surprises," the bishop said.

"I have never left this station," Doug replied, sounding a bit winded. "I am a prince here. Everyone knows me, and I know every corner of the place." He was smiling and regaining his breath as he said it, but there was a hint of sadness in his words. "If we had the time, I could show you a hundred more tricks like that."

"Have you ever wanted to leave?" Eddie asked.

"I was afraid," Doug said, still regaining his breath, "and I suppose I was encouraged to stay put. Or maybe 'manipulated to stay put' is a better way of phrasing it."

"You do not seem bitter about it," Mrs. Hemmer pointed out.

"I suppose I let myself be manipulated," Doug shrugged. "I went along with everyone's desire to keep me a kind of secret. As I said, I was afraid to leave. I had no friends away from here."

"I hope that we are friends," Eddie said.

"Yes, and soon to be brothers," Doug answered. His breath was coming more easily now.

"You know, I am free to travel," Eddie offered. "And I have a good deal of savings. Maybe we could take a trip together."

Doug held out his hand for Eddie to shake. "I have been having the same thought," he said.

The bishop was unsure about this. He had been meaning to talk with Eddie about the monks of Prince of Peace Abbey on the side of Mars' greatest mountain—Olympus Mons.

Eddie was a monk at heart; the bishop had grown fairly certain. He had already lived in a monastic manner as he worked freighters throughout the solar system. What he needed was a community to bring his vocation fully to life.

To travel with Doug—and the bishop could tell that Eddie's plan was to stay with Doug until death came—was a charitable idea, one the bishop could not help lauding. But was it where Eddie should be?

He smiled abstractly at the two friends as they shook on their plan, but before he could formulate anything to say, a gasping shriek interrupted.

Mrs. Hemmer was looking up toward one of the solar mirrors and covering her mouth in horror. The bishop easily followed the line of her gaze to the creature that had so shocked her.

It was pale, nearly translucent, and winged. It must have been five meters long and two or three wide. What made the creature frightening was that as huge and profoundly modified as it appeared, it had unmistakably human features: as if a human being had had been stretched to the very edge of recognizability.

Most frightening of all, however, was that the creature was not inside the station, but outside, clinging to the frame, and moving its way along as a lizard might. The bishop considered for a moment that it might be mechanical, some kind of robot, because, other than maybe some hardy bacteria, no bare and living thing could survive such exposure to airlessness and direct solar radiation.

But Doug quickly disabused him of any such notion. "It is a post-human," he said numbly. "It can survive for long periods in open space. I have seen them, even touched them. This station has produced scores of them in various shapes and sizes."

As Doug spoke, the creature folded itself into a thin and slithering thing and disappeared into a hatch.

"My God," the bishop said.

"Indeed," Doug answered.

# (25.)

Mr. Hemmer had had the good sense to capture video of the post-human. This the bishop sent via coded message to Rome, along with his own notes on the situation and a recording explaining his decision to baptize Doug.

The last bit was tricky. While it was obvious to the bishop that he was doing the right thing in baptizing Doug, it was not an area covered—at least as far as he knew—in Church law. Would the prelates in Rome agree with him? Would they scold him for not seeking advice before proceeding? Might they even inform him that he had been excommunicated?

Waiting for the return message to come, the bishop grew anxious. He really had no idea what things were like at the Vatican, at least not in any first-hand way, and having put himself in an awkward position, he now began to entertain various unpleasant possibilities.

What if the conspiratorial Father Van der Walt was right about the divisions within the Church? What if one of the cardinals rumored to be Fascist sympathizers were to get the message? A creature such as Doug could not be tolerated in the Fascist world. Rather than baptize him, a true Fascist would euthanize him or, at the very least, hide him away in some dark place. A prelate with such inclinations would be unlikely to look kindly on Doug's baptism.

On the other hand, what if the cardinal who got the message turned out to be a convinced New Progressivist? How might such a prelate politicize Doug? Doug could become a poster child for the New Progressivist idea of Church, a Church that encouraged humanity to strike out unfettered by old moralities in a thousand new directions at once?

When the message came, the bishop took a deep breath before reading it, and as he read he was immediately filled with a dread he had not, even in his anxiety, expected.

Apparently, whoever had received the message was neither a Fascist nor a New Progressivist, but an old-time traditionalist. The return message came under the seal of the Holy Father, and that, the bishop was fairly certain, meant it was from the Vatican Secretary of State or the Congregation for the Doctrine of the Faith or some similarly high office—no one else, the bishop thought, could seal a message with the papal seal.

There was much reference to mortal sin and the duty to preach the Gospel in season and out.

The only reference to Doug was to convey the Holy Father's apostolic blessing on the new brother and to order the bishop to see that once Doug was baptized he was given proper preparation to receive Confirmation, Eucharist, and the Sacrament of Reconciliation. If death became imminent, of course, the preparation was to be suspended in favor of immediate reception.

What was more, in his remaining time on the station, the bishop was to share the fullness of the Gospel with anyone on the station in a position of responsibility. He was to teach and instruct—in the most forceful manner—that human life was inviolable according to God's law, and that experiments using human creatures, no matter their condition, was to cease at once.

The bishop could hardly believe what he was reading. Of course he would see to Doug's religious education and initiation. That part was a relief. But what did this prelate think; the bishop could just give orders as if this were the Middle Ages? What was he to do, don the miter and crosier and command the board of the Melton Foundation to sackcloth and ashes? Should he insist that they kneel before him in the snow?

The bishop decided to take care of the easier duty first. He asked Doug and Eddie to meet him for lunch, and there he appointed Eddie as catechist to Doug. Eddie was to teach Doug the Faith, and to have him ready for the sacraments in nine months.

"I have sent the abbot at Prince of Peace Abbey on Mars a letter," the bishop told Eddie. "I have asked him to assign a priest to assist you. You are to check in with the assigned priest once a week and receive instruction on how you are to instruct Doug."

"I understand," Eddie said, but the bishop knew there was a good part of this arrangement that Eddie did not yet understand. The bishop was putting him in contact with the abbey for a reason. Perhaps Eddie would develop an interest in the monks.

To Doug, the bishop said, "In nine months at the latest, I expect to be home on Mars. If your travel plans allow it, come to Mars at that time, and I will finish your initiation into the Church. Do not fear for your soul, however. You will be baptized into Christ, and so long as you persevere in your love for him, you are assured of Heaven."

"I am just getting to know him," Doug said.

"That is true of all of us, Doug," the bishop replied. He was all business today. "Now, what are your plans for leaving Melton Station?"

"Actually, we are going to Mars," Eddie said. "The day after you leave here, there is a freighter coming into port that will head directly for Martian orbit."

"I want to walk on a real planet," Doug said somewhat sheepishly. "But I do not think I could handle two billion Earthlings yet, and it is too far to the Jovian colonies."

"So Mars it is," the bishop said with a smile. "Well, my ship is a cruise ship, some kind of entertainment barge that is making the grand tour of the solar system. They are on their way back to Earth from the Jovian moons. We depart at ten tomorrow morning. Would you both let me treat you to dinner tonight, and then, perhaps, see me off tomorrow?"

"We thought we would entertain you this afternoon with one last long stroll around the station," Eddie offered.

"There are still a few sights I would love to show you," Doug said.

"I'm sorry. I have some bishoping to do this afternoon, but thank you for the invitation. I will see you at dinner."

# (26.)

There were easier ways to get to B Dock, but Doug wanted Eddie to see the station's farms. So the two of them picked their way through the uneven ground of the Section Two pastureland.

"This was my favorite place to spend my days as a child," Doug said.

There were several dozen cattle in the field they crossed, a sight Eddie enjoyed. Near the middle of the pasture, they came upon an older man and woman working on a seeding project. They greeted Doug warmly.

"This is Maria and Nate; they run Section Two farming," Doug told Eddie.

Maria and Nate seemed genuinely upset to hear that Doug was leaving for Mars. They encouraged him, however, and said they completely understood his desire to see more of the world.

"Doug is a natural farmer," Maria told Eddie. "He has the touch."

"I believe it," Eddie said.

"I have just always loved it," Doug said. "I will really miss it, and I will miss both of you," he told Maria and Nate.

They hugged him and made him promise to keep in touch.

At the edge of the pasture, Eddie and Doug came to the Melton Station's main living area.

"Most of us live here," Doug said. "The houses set out in the country are nice, but living in town is better. I mean we're like 35 million miles from Earth, how isolated do you have to be?"

Doug pointed out the few sights of the town and then asked, "Do you mind if we make some more visits? There are people I want to say goodbye to."

"I don't mind at all," Eddie said.

For more than an hour Doug stopped by various offices and labs, introducing Eddie to long-time friends and saying his good-byes. Eddie found it exhausting, and was sure it must be even more so for Doug.

It came as a relief when finally they made it to the base of the Section Two B Dock elevator.

"Perhaps it is best that the bishop didn't join us for this particular adventure," Eddie said.

Doug laughed. "You might be right. From what he has told us, he seems best when he keeps his feet on the ground."

Melton Station was not much of a port of call, and it was rare for more than one ship to be docked at a time, so B Dock was rarely used. There was no one around as Doug and Eddie approached.

Doug tapped the glass of a small vendor and asked Eddie if he wanted some anti-nausea nasal spray before they went up.

Eddie, a long-time space farer, declined.

"I don't use it either," Doug said. "I must have done this a thousand times."

In the elevator, they slipped their feet into straps on the floor and asked for B Dock.

Because B Dock was at the center of the turning drum that was the Melton Station, it had no gravity.

When the doors opened, Eddie found himself following Doug out into a cylindrical room, grasping hand over hand the maneuvering grips that covered the walls.

It would have been very easy to become disoriented had there not been large block letters on each of the exits.

For example, on the doors facing them as they exited the elevator the letters read, "SECTION ONE ELEVATOR," and "SECTION THREE ELEVATOR."

To the left, there was a door with a sign that read B DOCK. To the right, another that read "VIEWING."

Eddie and Doug went right, and the door to the viewing deck opened for them as they approached.

Through it they could see the whole of the station's interior.

The viewing deck surprised Eddie because it was no more than a large metal frame covered in netting. Moving out into it, he felt an immediate sense of vulnerability. The station seemed an enormous barrel into which one might easily fall if suddenly gravity were to prove capricious.

The doors closed behind them, and Eddie found himself giddy with the strange feeling of being both high up and weightless. The A DOCK, nearly a kilometer away at the other end of the barrel, seemed to loom below, though there was, strictly speaking, no above or below here.

"I feel like I will fall," Eddie said, laughter in his voice.

"The experience of being at the zero-G center of a spinning station takes some getting used to," Doug replied.

The two of them laughed and floated about, moving around using the hand-over-hand method on the netting.

"You have to wear a harness to go out," Doug said.

Eddie's primitive brain was in a panic, and his higher brain was in a state of nearly pure delight. His mind could not reconcile the two experiences, so he began to giggle and soon found he could not suppress it.

Doug saw him and started to laugh, which was too much for Eddie, whose giggle erupted into a full-force snort, which set Doug off.

Eddie punched at the netting to try to stop the laugh, but in zero-G his punch became sort of a twisting flail that was so pathetic it set both he and Doug off laughing even harder.

They ended up lunging at each other and bouncing each other around the viewing area.

It took a long time for Eddie to breathe calmly again.

"Thanks," Doug said as he caught his breath. "I needed some cheering up."

Eddie frowned. "This is a hard day for you."

"Pretty hard," Doug said. "You still want to go out there?"

"I wouldn't miss it," Eddie said, the threat of another laugh eruption fully subsided now.

Doug opened a locker and pulled out two harnesses. He showed Eddie how to put his on and secure it. Ten meters of thin rope extended from the back of each harness. At the end of the ropes were clips that looked like something a mountaineer might use.

Doug showed Eddie how to coil his rope and hold it in his left hand as he made his way along the netting with his right until they got to the spot directly opposite the door they had entered by.

The netting could be pulled apart here, allowing them to move out into the station.

They did not move out, however, until Doug had attached the ends of both of their harness ropes to a taut line that ran from the metal framing out across the station.

"Its other end is all the way over at A Dock," Doug said.

"Have you ever gone all the way across?"

"Sure. There are several ways to do it, but let me show you the easiest one."

With that, Doug braced his feet against the outermost beam of the viewing area cage and pushed off. The angle of his push took him away from both the cage and the taut line until his own line reached its limit. At that point, Doug stopped. He did not bounce back. He just stopped.

He then called out, "Drone please," and there was a sudden buzzing on the wall behind Eddie.

Almost instantly a little drone came into view. With its propeller wrapped in a protective wire cage, it looked something like a flying room fan.

It flew to Doug, who caught it and began to maneuver himself around with it.

Doug's tether line went slack, and off he went, making loops around the taut line and moving away from Eddie toward the center of the station. At a short distance out, he turned and flew himself back to Eddie.

"Still want to try it?" he asked.

"What do you think?" Eddie said.

"OK, the first thing you should know is that your tether is made of nano-fiber that you control by gripping the chest-strap of your harness. Pull hard on it and the fiber locks in position. This keeps you from just bouncing around out of control. Let go and the fiber relaxes."

"And the second thing is that if you call for a drone, one will come. They're part of the recreation system built into the station."

Eddie found the system easy to master, and in a few minutes he and Doug had moved far out toward the center of the station.

Eddie marveled at the various tricks and spins that Doug had mastered. He did not try any of them himself, however. He was more than content just to let the little drone take him round and round the taut line as he enjoyed the awesome strangeness of the view.

Doug seemed free here, a master of his surroundings. Eddie enjoyed watching him fly and wondered, suddenly, whether leaving the Melton Station was the best plan.

# (27.)

At the bottom of the elevator, gravity returned, and on its heels, clarity.

The doors opened. Doug and Eddie stepped out, and waiting for them on a bench was a friendly-looking man of 60 or 65. His graying hair was tousled. He was dressed semi-casually with the collar of a white shirt poking out from under a black sweater.

He grinned awkwardly and waved a small wave at Doug as he stood up.

"Dr. Cantor," Doug exclaimed.

"I didn't want you to leave before I had a chance to talk with you."

"This is my friend Eddie Cho," Doug said. "Eddie, this is one of my oldest friends, Dr. Stephen Cantor."

Eddie and Dr. Cantor shook hands.

"So, you are leaving?" Dr. Cantor said. He had an awkward, distracted manner of speaking, as if he had a great deal on his mind.

"Yes," Doug said. "I have decided to travel with Eddie."

"I am sorry to hear that."

"Why?" Doug said. "I am happy with my choice."

"But you are sick, Doug. We have the facilities here to treat you."

"But not to keep me alive, I'm afraid."

"Not yet, Doug, but who knows, in a few months we might..."

"If you do, I can return for treatment."

"You seem very firm in your decision."

Doug did not answer, but smiled. Eddie thought the smile seemed slightly cold, as if to invite the doctor to let the topic drop. But the doctor did not.

"Doug, I want nothing more than your happiness, but leaving here cannot be in your best interest."

"I cannot imagine what would be more in my interest. I am going to see Mars, to see some of the wider world."

"And your new friends, have they helped convince you that this is the best course? You know, you hardly know them."

Eddie felt a slight heat of embarrassment at this, but was not sure if he was embarrassed for himself or for the doctor.

"I have made the decision for myself."

"Does this have something to do with religion, Doug? You know that these people might like to use you to try to discredit our work."

Now Eddie felt a heat that was not entirely embarrassment.

"I believe in God," Doug said.

The doctor shrugged as if to say, "These things happen. Even to intelligent people."

"I am sure that is not something you will find easy to understand. But no one has convinced me. And I have decided to go."

"I understand, Doug. Maybe more than you think I do. But there are things you are not considering. Have you considered your safety?"

Doug's head jerked slightly back at this. And he looked the doctor directly in the eyes.

"What about my safety?"

"There are people out there who might try to profit from your ... well, your novelty. Unscrupulous people. And there are people who might not be able to see your humanity. They might harm you. Here you are safe from all that."

"I don't think it will do any good to discuss this," Doug said.

"Doug, how can it hurt to discuss it? You are making a rash decision. Do you think the world outside of here is truly safe for you? You are influenced by your new friends."

"My...?" Doug seemed to be running short of words.

"I am sure they are fine people, but they have an agenda..."

"Let's discuss it then," Doug said. "I did not want to, but let's discuss my safety. When did you develop this tender concern for my safety?"

Eddie was surprised at the harsh tone of Doug's voice and apparently so was Dr. Cantor, who seemed entirely taken aback.

"We have always kept you safe, Doug. Why would you say such a thing? You are a valuable part of this community."

This seemed to hit Doug hard. For a moment he appeared dumbfounded. He shook his head, a look of pain on his face, as he stared wide-eyed at Dr. Cantor.

"But there was no one to keep me safe from you," he said. His voice cracked as he said it, and tears began to flow.

"If someone has hurt you, I am sorry. Truly, I am sorry. But we did our very best to keep you safe."

Doug could not contain himself anymore. He rose up and shouted in the face of the kindly doctor.

"Then where are my arms and legs? Where is my face? What did you do with it? You threw it away."

"Doug I..."

"I have never seen my own face," Doug yelled. "You stole everything from me."

Doug sat down and sobbed into his long hands. Dr. Cantor looked down at him with sympathy.

"I am sorry, Doug, that you are leaving," he said. "And I am even sorrier that we are parting on these terms. I would prefer we had parted friends. I think we could help you, if you chose to stay. You sound depressed. Well, there are treatments for depression. It does not have to be this way."

And when he had said it, he turned and walked away.

Eddie stood alone and watched the doctor leave, unsure how to comfort Doug, but certain now that Doug should not stay here.

"How can a person be so blind, so unwilling to see?" Doug looked up and implored Eddie.

"I don't know," Eddie said.

Doug shook his head. He did not seem sad anymore, but bitter, as if he wanted to spit the whole Melton Station out of his mouth.

# (28.)

The truth was that the bishop was not at all sure how to undertake the afternoon's remaining duty. He had been instructed to preach. But where? There was no Aereopagus. In fact, the bishop could not remember seeing a single large gathering place.

The people of Melton Station had their entertainments, but gathering together as a community did not seem to be part of their life.

He could go to the Red Barn and just wander around talking to people about God. That might even be pleasant. But he had been expressly instructed to preach to those in positions of responsibility, and he had no idea who that might be.

No official delegation had ever greeted the bishop or his fellow travelers. No one had bothered them, but neither had anyone really welcomed them. They were free to visit, to rent rooms, to enjoy meals, and to stroll anywhere they liked.

But there must be leaders, mustn't there? The place must have some structure.

He decided to go back to the beginning, to see if Sailor the lion and the young woman who greeted newcomers might still be around. He would ask the young woman if she could tell him who ran the station and where he could find them. But when he got back to the elevator, neither she nor Sailor was anywhere to be found.

He followed the winding trail back to the Red Barn.

Not sure what else to do, he asked the Barn's reception hologram, "Can you tell me who runs the Melton Station?"

The hologram began explaining the Melton Foundation and its goals.

"But who runs it?" the bishop asked.

"The Melton Foundation is a private foundation with decision-making authority vested in a board of twelve directors."

"Can you tell me the names of the board members and where I can find them?"

The holo displayed a list of twelve names, all PhDs or MDs. The bishop recognized none of them.

"I am not permitted to share the locations of individuals," the holo said.

"Can you tell me whether they are on the station?"

"No, sir, I cannot."

"I understand. Thank you," the bishop said, and he decided to return to his room to think things over. Perhaps there was some way to get in touch with one of the board members. That would be a start. On his way to his room, however, he had another thought. Why not just ask a living person? Just walk up to someone shopping or dining in the Barn and ask how he might find the board of directors.

He tried three different people. Each was a visitor from off station, and none had any idea how to help.

He said a little prayer to St. Anthony and headed once again back to his room. He would rest and think for a while about what step to take next.

But as he approached his room, he could see that no rest was likely. Two men were waiting outside his door, sitting on folding chairs.

"Gentlemen," he called out as he approached, "can I help you?"

"Bishop Mark Gastelum?"

"Yes."

"We were starting to think you weren't coming back," they grumbled. "The Melton Board of Directors is meeting all this week on the station. They have asked for you to attend this afternoon's meeting, if it is not inconvenient."

The bishop had an odd sensation.

In his experience, when signs begin to pile up— orders from the Vatican to preach, and then the very people he was trying find reaching out to find him—an effort larger than his own was being made.

"Not at all," the bishop laughed. "I'd be delighted."

"We can wait if you need to get anything from your room."

"I don't think I'll be needing a staff or a bag or an extra tunic," the bishop joked.

The two men clearly did not get the reference, but they laughed politely.

Together, the three took a path that the bishop had been down several times on his various strolls. If they kept following it, the bishop knew, it would meander through some fields and eventually up the side of the station and onto a catwalk that crossed one of the three great windows.

But they did not keep following it. At a nondescript bend in the path, the two escorts stopped and touched one of the decorative wooden fences. It slid open to reveal another path, this one leading toward a cluster of larger buildings that the bishop took to be a lab complex.

At this moment he realized that none of the paths he had walked ever took him near to lab buildings. The design of the paths was so subtle that he had never felt himself being kept away from labs. Rather, he simply assumed that he could have gone to them had he wanted.

But now he was not so sure.

The openness and liberty of the Melton Station began to seem just another illusion that its designers had built in.

Once behind the fence, the path led downward into a well-lit tunnel. This went on for maybe fifty meters and then emerged into a hyper-modern square amid five large buildings.

"This way," one of the escorts said, and the bishop was led to the smallest of the five buildings. There seemed to be little security, though the trio was scanned twice as they made their way to the boardroom.

Outside the boardroom was the same young woman who, with Sailor the lion, had greeted guests upon arrival at the station.

"I'm Kendra," she said. "We met once before, when you arrived."

"I remember," the bishop answered. "But where is Sailor today?"

"Ah, you do remember," Kendra said happily. "Sailor has the day off and is probably wandering the hills of Section 1."

"Lucky lion," the bishop said.

"Well, first of all, thank you for coming," she said, getting down to business. "This is sort of a providential coincidence, I think. The Foundation Board is meeting all this week. They have come in from Earth, mostly, but several live on station and a few more are from other stations. One of their agenda items is an issue with the Christian churches. And when members found out that a Catholic bishop was on station, they thought it opportune to invite you in for a dialogue."

"I see," the bishop said, "I am honored that they would invite me." He wondered if she knew what the word "providential" meant.

"They should be back in session in about a half hour," Kendra said. "Can I offer you anything while you wait?"

"A quiet place to say my prayers, if you have it."

"Um, yes, do you need any special..?"

"A chair, if you've got one."

"Sure, I guess, well, let me put you in the small conference room."

The room was octagonal with an octagonal center table, eight chairs, and a few side tables: very sparse, sleek.

"Perfect," the bishop said as they entered, and this seemed to relieve Kendra of some anxiety.

"Would you like to pray with me?"

For a moment he was certain that Kendra was about to say yes, but she did not.

"I'm sorry. I have things I have to get to," she said pleasantly, and she left him alone.

# (29.)

The bishop's comcom projected his breviary onto his hands, and he began to read his prayers. His mind wandered almost immediately. He had always had a problem with daydreaming during prayer. Often, he would daydream away more than half a rosary before his mind would settle down and simply pray. One of the difficulties with overcoming daydreaming during prayer, he found, was that it could go on for quite a while before he even noticed it was happening.

As he read the words, his mind wandered back to the Fuhrer and his plans for war. Places like the Melton Station would be torn apart if that war came. Creatures such as Doug and the post-human they had seen clawing its way along the outside of the station would be burned up in the fires of the Fascist conflagration. Even Sailor would be killed—a symbol of the softness and flabbiness of the New Progressivists. The glory of real lions, red in tooth and claw, would be restored. The solar system—every station, every colony, every city, town, and family—would be purged and purified. The sick healthfulness of the Fascists would reign everywhere—made constant by murder.

The bishop saw the Fuhrer striding onto the Melton Station and railing against its replacement of real human glory with the false glory of the intellectuals, the false glory of moral confusion. He saw the executions and the terror and the betrayals—the scientists and technicians who would sell out their fellows and join the Fascists just to stay alive.

Certainly, part of him took bitter pleasure in the shock that the Fascists would bring, and the force they would exert to stop the grotesqueries of this inhuman place. The New Progressivists would never be able to see that they, themselves—with their rejection of reality and their willingness to break almost any boundary—had given fuel to the fire of the New Fascism.

People know—in their souls they know—when moral sickness becomes ascendant, and they rebel, often irrationally, in an attempt to restore health to society.

Today, millions upon millions of people turned to the Fascists not because it was innate for them to do so, but because they were sickened by the libertinism and self-righteousness of the New Progressivists.

The father of Fascism is nostalgia, and the New Progressivists had created a powerful swell of nostalgia for simpler times and cleaner living by their unremitting moral outrages and their unwillingness to suffer any limit.

The bishop was agitated by his daydream and arose from it feeling ashamed at his neglect of prayer. For a moment, he gave up. He thought about what he would say to the Melton Board but could come up with nothing.

He gathered himself for another attempt at prayer and began the Our Father.

He was still agitated when Kendra returned and said the board was ready for him.

She escorted him to a larger and brighter room where twelve people were seated around an outsized table. They rose as the bishop entered, offered their hands, and introduced themselves.

The bishop was offered a chair, and the meeting was called to order.

The board had asked him to meet with them because they wanted to explain the good work they were doing and to ask about gaining more support from the Church for a new work they were about to embark on.

They felt they could offer people wildly extended life spans and profound new abilities to fight disease, to explore the solar system, and maybe even to live for long periods comfortably in the thin atmosphere of Mars.

The bishop thanked them for their willingness to dialogue, and suggested they establish a formal dialogue with the Vatican, a process he would be happy to suggest to the pope when they met in a few months. However, he felt he had to be honest with them about the moral problems the Church would have with some of their work.

"We just feel that if you understood the science, there would be less emotional resistance," one member said.

The bishop was pinned to his seat by these words. How could one engage with people who saw moral objections simply as "emotional resistance"?

He did not know how, but he found himself speaking to them, instead, about the wonder of the world and the great gift humanity possessed in its ability to explore the world through science.

"But humanity must also explore the world through other means. Our sense that the world makes sense is correct," he said. "If it were not correct, science itself could not work. The nihilists and the V-junkies and the many different kinds of indifferent people are all wrong when they say the world is senseless and unknowable.

"But what is also knowable is that the human being is not like anything else in the universe; it is a creature of strange nobility and value. Each human being is a universe unto itself, valuable beyond measure.

"And you must stop your destruction, your instrumentalization, of human lives. It is morally unbearable. I demand in the name of the Most Holy God that you stop it, repent, and make right the damage you have done!"

The bishop was not sure how it had happened, but he was standing. He had raised his hands as he shouted out the last few sentences.

He was shocked and amazed at his own words. Who was he to command these people? What had he done? They had asked for dialogue, and he had rained down fire on their heads.

One woman rose and stomped out of the room. Others looked at him with either sympathy or horror or some combination of emotions that he could not decipher.

"Thank you, bishop," the chairman said. "We appreciate your very frank words. We will give them a great deal of thought."

Things went on like that for a few moments as they dismissed him and, finally, closed the door behind him.

His head felt hollow, and his breath was thin.

"How did everything go?" the bright voice of Kendra called out down the hall.

"I'm afraid not so well," the bishop said, gathering himself.

"I'm sorry to hear that," Kendra said, her voice losing none of its insistent brightness. "Will you be needing an escort back to your quarters?"

"No," the bishop said. "I think I would prefer just to walk alone."

"Absolutely," Kendra said. "Thank you so much for coming."

# (30.)

The bishop did not make it to the public path alone, however. As he stepped out of the building and into the plaza, he saw the woman who had stomped out of the meeting. She was sitting on the steps of another building a short distance away.

The bishop saw her just a moment before she saw him, and he thought for that moment that he might pass her without incident. All he wanted was to make it back to his room and be alone.

He felt as foolish as he had ever felt in his life.

But she saw him, and when she did, she did not hesitate. She arose at once and came after him.

He kept walking but prepared himself for the attack. *He was a bigot, and he had no right to talk to people that way. This is what made people hate religion, self-righteous and overbearing jerks like him.*

The familiarity of the verbal assault would not make it easier to endure.

There would probably be some reference made to the Catholic hatred of sex and of women and of science and ... he steeled himself.

He could see tears of rage streaming down her face as she approached.

He tried offering a welcoming smile.

And without warning she grabbed him.

Her arms went under his arms and wrapped around his chest. Her cheek pressed into him right above his heart. She held on fiercely.

And she wept.

He said no word to her but stood uncomprehending, looking around the plaza as if for help.

Sobbing, she begged, "Forgive me, father."

The tone of her voice said more, even, than did her words. There would be no attack. Some plan seemed to be coming to fruition, but he did not know whose. Had someone at the Vatican known about her? Was that possible? Was it true what some people said, that the Vatican had spies everywhere? Was it for her sake that he was sent to preach?

"Are you a Catholic?" he asked her, and this question brought a whole new wave of sobbing.

"I was baptized Russian Orthodox," she said, "but I have not ever practiced it."

"I see," he said. "Would you like to make a confession?" He was not familiar with the Russian Orthodox Rite of Reconciliation, but—as a Catholic— he was in full communion with them, and could offer her absolution.

She knelt, and, though it was awkward in the middle of the plaza, he knelt with her and heard her confession.

Her name was Ovca.

"There was a preacher who came here a few years ago, and he explained the Christian faith to me in a way I had never heard it. It has been tugging at my heart ever since, and when you said to stop what we are doing here, it hit my heart very hard. I knew you were right, and I knew that this is what God has been calling me to."

"I see," the bishop said. Words were pouring out of her, and she had no idea how to make a confession, so he interrupted here and there to help her through.

It took a long time, and his knees ached by the time he pronounced absolution. In the course of her confession he learned a good deal about what went on in the labs around him. Some of it was mild; some of it was grotesque even beyond what he already knew. He learned that the human-like creature that had crawled along the outside of the station had no brain but was run using an installed computer. Separate experiments were being done on hardening human brains against radiation and transplanting them into post-human bodies.

After absolution the bishop assured her that she truly was forgiven.

"That is all it takes?" she asked.

"For our part, yes," he said.

She helped him up off his knees. He asked her if she would walk with him back to the Red Barn. Ovca wrapped her arm around his, and they walked together.

He wanted to talk more with her then but was exhausted. Instead, he told her briefly about Doug and Eddie and the Hemmers, asking if she would join them all for dinner.

Ovca knew Doug and was thrilled to hear about his baptism. She wanted to speak with him, and apologize for having tolerated the injustices done against him.

"Until then," the bishop said tiredly, and took his leave.

# (31.)

The water in the little streams of the Melton Station did not come from Earth. It was too expensive to lift water from Earth and bring it this far out.

It might have come from a comet. Several had been captured and mined for their water, which was then sold to station colonies. But more likely it came from Ceres or one of the other asteroid belt objects. Many of them were little more than big, dirty chunks of ice. They had circled the sun for a billion years or so until some ship grabbed them out of space and brought them, more precious than gold out here, to slake the thirst of yet another human colony.

The bishop had a little shell that had been given to him as a gift at his ordination. It was a real shell from one of the seas of Earth, and its edges were gilt.

With his little shell he had stepped down into the stream that flowed by the Red Barn.

His white vestments were immediately soaked up to his chest, and it was cold.

The Hemmers and Ovca remained standing on the shore and the sun shone above as Eddie helped Doug into the water.

Doug leaned back, entrusting himself to Eddie and the bishop.

Three times the bishop dipped the shell into the water and poured it over Doug's head.

"I baptize you, Doug, in the name of the Father ... and of the Son ... and of the Holy Spirit..."

After the last of the three pourings, the bishop handed the shell to Eddie and took Doug into his own arms. He pushed Doug under the water, and Doug laid back, his eyes open and looking up at the bishop.

Doug did not struggle or resist but waited to be raised up by a power that was not his own.

Ovca wept when Doug came up out of the stream to give her the kiss of peace. Doug knew why she wept. She had been brought up out of the waters of death, too.

"Peace, sister," he said as he kissed her.

"Peace, brother," she said, hugging his still-wet body close to her and adding her tears to his baptismal waters.

# (32.)

For the first few days on the cruise ship Bacchanal, the bishop more or less confined himself to quarters. After the many shocks of the Melton Station, and after the emotional good-byes with Doug and Eddie, and then with Ovca and the Hemmers (who had agreed to travel with Ovca to a station hospital where she thought she might find work), the bishop had hoped for a quiet ship full of elderly tourists. The Bacchanal was about as far from that hope as one could get.

The ship was enormous, the largest unregistered passenger ship in the solar system. It was perhaps seven or eight times the size of the Frank Sinatra, but without any of the Sinatra's elegance. Its patrons were young and rich and in the midst of a three-year tour of the solar system. They were free to go wherever they wanted and do whatever they wanted, and a gaudy, unregistered ship was just the thing for the kind of libertine adventure they were after.

Their first stop had been Mars, and then they had travelled out as far as Callisto, where they had stayed for three months, taking side trips to several of the Jovian colonies. From there they had made their way back down toward the inner solar system, hopping from one asteroid belt station to another.

They had, of course, skipped Ceres.

Now they were headed to Earth, where they would remain for several months in orbit before making visits to Venus and to the colonies at each of the major Earth-Sun Lagrange points.

From his first moments on the ship, the bishop got the strong sense that, while the grand tour was all well and good, the real purpose of the trip was simply to enjoy a three-year party.

He was going to be spending forty days on the Bacchanal in transit to the moon. He allowed himself a few days of isolation before trying to cope with the constant party atmosphere.

He posted an offer on the ship's net to celebrate daily Mass but got no takers. So he celebrated Mass alone each morning, ate breakfast in his room, and devoted himself to communications with his diocese on Mars until lunch.

At lunch he would venture out into the common areas—casinos, dining rooms, sports courts, media rooms, more casinos, more dining rooms, menageries, and on and on. To the side of one casino, the bishop found a relatively quiet sandwich counter called The Octopus. A remarkably human-like androbot took orders and handed them to a man-sized robotic octopus, which assembled up to five sandwiches at once.

The bishop liked the place. It had tables in the back that were quiet and out of the way. Each day he intended to read while he ate, but found himself ignoring his reader as he watched the young people of the Bacchanal.

They were almost universally friendly and enthusiastic. Even after nearly two full years of travel, there seemed to be no boredom in them. Groups of friends would gather, run through ideas for the day, settle on some plan, and set off together as excitedly as children setting off for an amusement park.

And they were pampered like children, as well. The ship had a huge contingent of androbots, all extraordinarily lifelike. They were so beautifully human in their appearance and so willing to serve even the smallest needs of the passengers that the bishop began to think of them as post-modern recreations of ancient Roman slaves.

They were not androids, of course. They had no real intelligence. True machine consciousness remained a technical impossibility, a dream of technophiles and scientists ever over the horizon.

But these androbots had such subtle mimicry of both the physical and conversational skills of humans that they could easily be mistaken for human in many circumstances.

Even the pampering and the endless entertainment—as impressive as they were, however—could not possibly have kept the Bacchanal's passengers so free of boredom, so preternaturally interested and eager. Not even the cleverest designer drugs could do that, which is why the ship was stocked with an almost inexhaustible supply of nano-V.

The passengers were friendly and fervent because the V kept them that way.

It did not make people drowsy or obnoxious or paranoid. It did not give them hangovers or keep them chasing a high. From what the bishop had been told, it simply magnified good experiences and minimized bad.

In fact, only three negative side effects had ever been noticed among V-users. First, people who took nano-V tended to want to keep taking it. Second, those on V for long periods tended not to maintain close relationships. And third, people on V tended to stop living what are usually referred to as "productive lives."

None of these problems seemed particularly relevant to the rich young people of the Bacchanal. They were all on V, and none of them needed jobs.

Had they taken any interest in the bishop, he might have tried to tell them that there is much more to life than entertainment, but they did not take any interest, nor would they, nor would such an argument likely have meant much to them.

In their way of seeing things, life was pure gift— a notion the bishop also believed in. But in his world, the gift of life came from God, and its fulfillment could only be had in friendship with God. In theirs, the gift was an accident. It came from the chance combination of some lucky organic molecules billions of years ago. It was meaningless, and it was brief. What could make more sense than simply enjoying it to the full?

As much as he liked the young people of the Bacchanal, he felt intensely alone among them. They were on the other side of a chasm from him.

After a while, he began to take lunches in his room, and dinners.

# (33.)

The bishop tried to keep up his work but found it increasingly difficult to focus. He began to sleep in and avoid calls to Mars. He left letters unwritten and felt entirely dry—even bored—in his prayer life.

He was familiar with this ache, this dull misery, and he knew he had to fight the descent into depression.

But he was alone among these vapid young for another month. The thought of it pressed down on him. Everything pressed down on him.

He had always thought of his priestly life as important, a thought that was implicitly confirmed when he was made a bishop. But for the first time he was having trouble seeing how it mattered at all. How did anything matter?

"Humanity is lost."

The thought rose up in him several times a day. Each time it rose, he repented of it. It was such an evil and faithless idea. But he could not fight the feeling that—faithless as it may be—it was essentially correct.

He found himself secretly wishing for the Fascist wave to break, for war to come.

He fought the wish, and offered prayers that it would not come.

But a purifying fire was needed. Humanity needed to be woken up.

"I am depressed," he told himself. He knew from experience how dangerous depression could be, that these dark thoughts would not lead to light but, instead, would lead down and down and down into ever thicker darkness.

He bore it for more than a week, but then, nearing desperation, he spoke to the Bacchanal's ShipDoc.

The ShipDoc ran through the usual battery of psychiatric questions, blood tests, and quizzes.

"You have a genetic predisposition to depression," it told him. "Have you been depressed before?"

"Yes, I have. Twice it became very serious," the bishop answered.

"What treatment did you receive?"

"Neuro-synaptic recovery."

"It was effective?"

"Yes."

"I am not equipped for such a procedure," ShipDoc said. "But there are other therapies available."

"What are my options?"

"You can receive neuro-synaptic recovery therapy when we reach the moon. Because it has been effective, I would recommend that. I could provide chemical supports for the duration of the trip."

The bishop inhaled deeply. The thought of taking drugs was unappealing to him.

"Or we can insert nanites. This would stabilize you until we reach the moon."

"Do you mean nano-V?"

"That is the common designation, yes."

The bishop knew he should have said no right away. He could make it to the moon. It would hurt, but he could make it. If it got too bad, he could take the drugs.

"What are the side effects?" he asked.

"Short term supervised use of V-nanites has no known side effects."

"If I decide to, how do we proceed?"

"You will need to be sedated for about an hour. I will scan your nervous system, program the nanites, and insert them. When you awake you will feel better. If you would like to proceed, I will read you the disclaimer."

"Well. It's ... yes. OK, just let me hear the disclaimer."

"Your response is being recorded—The treatment being prescribed is for the short-term treatment of major depression. It is not a drug therapy. It will require that your nervous system is scanned using microscopic internal probes. These scans will allow the programming of molecule-sized machines. These machines will be injected into your bloodstream and directly into your nervous-system tissues, including the tissues of your brain. These machines—called nanites—will monitor and assist your nervous system and brain tissues. This personally programmed nanite treatment has been shown to improve mood and increase overall wellbeing and enjoyment. Nanites are highly effective for the short-term treatment of clinical depression. Do you understand this description?"

"Yes."

"Do you consent to the prescribed treatment?"

"Yes."

"Please lie down."

*Water is beautiful, and it made him laugh.*

The ShipDoc said, "Are you feeling better?"

The bishop said, "I am still waking up."

"Of course," the ShipDoc said. He had a nice voice. "Would you like a cool drink of water?"

*Water is beautiful. The taste of it is perfection. He could think of no word but perfection. It was like a living thing, a spirit, in his mouth. He swirled the remainder around in the cup and watched it spin.*

"Beautiful," he said.

"I do feel better," he told the ShipDoc. "May I go?"

"I would prefer you stay just a few minutes for observation."

"Great," the bishop said. It was very comfortable in the exam room.

*What is the difference between comfortable and uncomfortable? The exam table is warm.*

*Warm is comfortable until it is hot or until you have had enough of warm.*

*What, really, does "enough" mean? "Enough" is a funny word. "Enough" is the word for you when you have had enough.*

"You can control the nanites," ShipDoc told him, "simply by using your own implant computer."

The bishop liked the way ShipDoc said, "implant."

*Did they program ShipDoc with an accent? Everybody but the Amish got the implant. How else would you access the Web? How else would you function in the world?*

*The world, the world.*

*There are two worlds—the world of immediacy and the world mediated by meaning.*

*That is what they taught us in seminary.*

"Just bring up the nanite app and adjust it," ShipDoc told him. "Up means experiences will be greatly intensified and pleasurable. Down means you will get less of a boost. Just remember that if you are tuned up too high, your thoughts may feel like they are racing."

The bishop opened the app and found it had defaulted to the highest setting. He turned it down. Instantly, he felt more like himself, less thrilled by every little thing.

"Thank you," he told the ShipDoc. "I think I am fine now. I am going to go."

"Would you come back tomorrow just for a five minute follow-up?"

"Yes," the bishop said, but he had the sudden idea to go back to his room and watch media. He never really liked media so much, but he wanted to try it with the V turned up.

# (34.)

The bishop did not go back to his room, however. Once out of ShipDoc's office, he found himself suddenly enchanted by the Bacchanal's many offerings.

He understood now. The ship wasn't gaudy; it was playful and ironic. The lights, the music, the decorations, the furniture, the androbots—it all worked together as a kind of silly commentary on post-modern culture.

He sat down at a casino card table and played for several hours. He was able to concentrate on his cards with no problem, even as he kept up several conversations at once. The two young couples at the table were lively and friendly, and they told many hilarious and outrageous stories of the trip so far.

They told him that they had just spent a week plugged-in.

He smiled and nodded at that. He told the dealer to give him a card.

"You don't know what 'plugged-in' means, do you?" one of the women asked.

The bishop had nineteen, and the dealer was showing a six. He signaled to stay pat.

"Not the slightest idea," he said with a broad smile.

All four of his new friends found this wildly funny.

The dealer busted.

"Well, what is it?" he asked.

"It's really the original reason that nano-V was invented," they told him. "It allows for super-realistic media experiences. You should try it."

"How would I try it?"

"Ask one of the androbots to help you."

The bishop played a few more hands of cards and then thanked them all for a pleasant afternoon.

When he got back to his room, he showered and then turned on a holo-film, one of the pulp action blockbusters that he had never really had time for.

He turned up his V as far as it would go. The opening shot was a fly-over of Tokyo. The camera rose and fell as it barely cleared the tops of the city's buildings.

He was flying.

With the V, the sensation was terrifying and gripping. He laughed out loud.

He watched the entire film without moving, and when it was over, he searched through the files for another film of the same type.

He was still watching films when morning came.

Several times his V app had tried to convince him to sleep, but he was beyond convincing. Now the app insisted. It informed him that safety precautions were built into the system to protect users. The bishop felt suddenly heavy.

He crawled his way up the bed and collapsed on a pillow.

Exactly eight hours later he awoke, feeling as good as he had ever felt.

There is no harm in this, he told himself. It was prescribed for a legitimate medical need in a controlled setting. He would stay on the V just until he got to the moon and then seek treatment.

For now, why not make the most of the experience?

He called for an androbot.

"Please explain to me how I plug in."

"Certainly sir," it said. It was feminine and beautiful and charming.

Why did they make the androbots so beautiful? And what was the extent of their services?

The V made it very hard for the bishop to feel disturbed by even these questions.

The androbot led him to a non-descript doorway just a few doors down from his own room. Behind the door were a little lobby and six other doors. The androbot opened one and motioned for him to follow. Behind the door was a small box of a room, about three meters to a side.

There was nothing in it. The floor, ceiling, and walls were heavily padded in a substance that the bishop had never seen or felt before.

"This is an adventure room," the androbot said. "When people speak of being plugged in, they are referring to a room like this."

"How does it work?"

"Though you cannot see them, there are several top of the line entertainment tools embedded within this room. The most important of these is a super-high-resolution pyramidal projector. In layman's terms, that means a holo-projector that surrounds the user. When it is on, the room we are in disappears and the user is fully enclosed within a high-resolution 3D representation. Then there is a high-resolution sound system, a full-spectrum air system, and malleable surfaces. Do you need me to explain these?"

"Just the last two."

"The full-spectrum air system will allow for the introduction of smells, the sensation of motion, and real flight. That is to say, the air can be circulated in such a manner that the user leaves the ground and is held suspended in flight."

"I see."

"The malleable surface system allows the walls to take on various shapes and textures that can be synchronized with the visual projector."

"I see," the bishop said again.

"We have an introductory presentation. Would you like to try it?"

"Yes."

"Please lie down."

The androbot left the room, and the bishop turned the V up to full. He found he enjoyed the anticipation, though nothing seemed to happen for several minutes.

And then far off there was the sound of waves. At first he was not even sure that he was hearing it, but little by little it grew.

They were real waves. He could smell them. The ocean breeze was light and salty. He turned to look and far off he could see the ocean, the sea itself. The vast sea and the vast sky. Between him and the ocean were dunes and beach-grass and a wooden fence beside a wooden path.

He turned his head to look back into the room. But there were more dunes there, more grass, and more fences.

He sat up.

The dunes and the sea and the sky—each in its own place—went on forever.

This was fine. He would stay here forever. Everything was so bright, so peaceful.

There were two children on the beach.

He waved to them.

They waved and came toward him along the wooden path.

"Hello," they said.

"Hello."

One was a girl, and one was a boy. They seemed about ten or eleven.

"You are plugged in now," the boy said.

"I assumed so," the bishop said.

"You can turn off the system at any time by touching your two middle fingers to your thumbs like this," the girl told him.

He did not try it.

"And you can bring up a menu at any time by touching the tips of your left-hand digits to the tips of your right-hand digits, like this," the boy said.

The bishop tried it, and a menu appeared just above his hands.

"Fold your hands like this to make the menu disappear," the girl said. She folded her fingers flatly over the palms of her two hands. The bishop tried it, and the menu disappeared.

For the next several minutes, the two children explained his options to him. He could create his own world by bringing up the menu and telling it what he wanted. He could run pre-programmed scenarios such as swimming with whales or flying over the Himalayas or touring Paris.

Or he could run stories. The computer had an almost inexhaustible supply of them. They would run much like a film, but he would be inside the film, living it.

When they were done explaining, the children told him that he could access them any time he needed simply by bringing up the menu and pressing the "HELP" button.

With that, they were gone, and he was alone, a god in his own world.

# (35.)

The bishop soon discovered how it was possible for the young people he had played cards with to spend a week plugged in. If you became hungry, you could open the menu and order food. It was not holo-food, but real food. An androbot would carry a tray into whatever world you happened to be in. On the tray would be the food you had ordered.

And if you got tired, you could sleep on a beach in a hammock, or in the king's bed at Versailles, or floating among the stars with galaxies spinning around you.

The bishop was sure that without the V, the experience of one of these rooms would be exhilarating. But with the V, it was beyond description. He decided to stay the night and then the next day.

He explored the surface of his own home planet without pressure suit or helmet. He ventured out to the Jovian colonies and beyond, all the way to the new outposts around Saturn. He thought of visiting Jerusalem or St. Peter's Basilica, but decided that would have to wait until he was on the real Earth.

He watched several films, but "watched" was not the right word; "participated in" would be a better description.

He decided to stay another day and another night.

And then another.

Some of the stories he participated in were not meant for a bishop. But something about the V made it almost impossible to resist temptation.

Though he felt as awake and alert as ever, he felt unlike himself. He was not much bothered by conscience, for one thing.

On some level that seemed to be below his emotions, this loss of contact with himself was uncomfortable. "This is not right," he thought on several occasions. But though he could know it was not right, he could not feel it. And without feeling, much of the motivation for corrective action was missing.

He passed from place to place, from adventure to adventure. They streamed over him in an exciting torrent, and the V within him made the experiences real, irresistibly real.

His mind remained clear and sharp. Sharper than ever, in fact. And that may have been what saved him from simply floating away and disappearing in a river of perfected experiences.

He thought of Mars. He remembered his vows.

He never was able to say what convinced him to do it, but on the fourth day he touched the tips of his middle fingers to the tips of his thumbs, and in an instant it was all gone. He was standing in a padded room, staring at a door.

He felt good. The V was working. The V always worked. But he had calls to make to Mars; he had work to get done. He remembered his ethics instructor telling him that being human comes with two innate directives—be reasonable, and be responsible.

He stared at the door. He made a decision. He was going to leave now, get to his work. And then even as he made that decision he decided that a few more hours would not hurt. He wanted to ride elephants.

He was about to turn the system back on when the door opened.

"You turned the system off," an androbot said.

The presence of the androbot was too human. Somewhere within himself, despite the V, he felt ashamed.

"Yes. I have work to get done."

He turned the V down to the minimum, headed back to his room, and showered. He ordered breakfast and ate quietly. For a while he felt fairly normal and was able to work.

But he wanted to talk to a real person. He found he needed to talk with a real person. He needed conversation to clean a film of dreams off, to return to the real.

He wished there were another priest on the Bacchanal to hear his confession.

And then he remembered Mass.

He had not celebrated it for several days. He had not prayed or even thought much about God. Quickly, before he could talk himself out of it, he asked the ship's computer to find him the nearest Catholic priest.

The computer found a Jesuit on a station that was currently only about half a million miles away. That would mean a communications delay of only about two seconds.

"Please call him for me," the bishop said.

He read his hours while he waited, and in less than ten minutes the Jesuit was on the line. The bishop explained the situation to him starting with the depression and ending with his failure to celebrate Mass for several days.

"Did you take the V to treat the depression, or did you use the depression as an excuse?" the Jesuit asked gruffly.

"Father, I am not certain, but I am sure that some part of me wanted to try it."

"OK, bishop, is there anything else you want to tell me?"

"No, but I want to be sure you understand that some of the films were ... prurient."

"Yes. You made that clear. I think you have accused yourself adequately."

This Jesuit was businesslike. All he wanted were the facts of the matter: no false sorrow but no excuses, either.

"Bishop, it seems to me that your illness really is a mitigating factor. You went to the ShipDoc for help when you were vulnerable, and maybe you could have said no to the V, but you were not required to say no. It also seems to me that you are under some stress, and you are alone. You have heard enough confessions to know what happens to people when we are under stress and alone. Bishops as much as anyone else. To put it succinctly, I don't think there's a mortal sin here, but I do think you should seek absolution once you get to the moon. Do you think you can stay away from near occasions until then?"

"Yes, Father, I do."

"I would suggest some kind of penance. Do you have any ideas?"

"I could go off the V and just live with the depression for the next weeks."

"No," the Jesuit said, "I don't think we'd better do that. Your mental health is not something to play around with. How about you agree to keep the V at the lowest setting and give up all entertainment media until you get the V out of your system on the moon."

"Yes, Father. Thank you for your help."

"Certainly bishop. Call back if you need me. Now bow your head and pray for God's blessing."

The bishop bowed.

"I cannot absolve you of your sins at this time because, as you know, no confession is valid unless the priest is present to the penitent. However, in the name of the One, Holy, Catholic, And Apostolic Church, I offer you conditional absolution, so long as you make a sincere effort to confess your sins the next time a priest is available to you. Go in peace, my brother, in the name of the Father, and of the Son, and of the Holy Spirit."

The bishop did not feel the kind of relief and peace he usually felt at the end of confession. Still, he knew intellectually what he could not currently know emotionally: all was forgiven.

"Amen," he said.

# (36.)

The cities of the moon were much more impressive than those on Mars. They spread out like spider webs across the surface, and some had dozens of common areas each as big as Coolidge-town. The underground habitations must have been massive.

Waiting for a ride to the surface from the Bacchanal, the bishop gazed down at passing towns, roads, mines, and factories. He tried to pick out familiar sights but found it difficult to get his bearings while traveling so quickly over the surface.

In the distance he could make out passing orbital stations from time to time, and for a moment he caught sight of a massive ship under construction. Because of the distance, he could not be sure of its size, but it seemed quite a few times larger even than the Bacchanal.

Was it a war ship?

The V, even at low power, kept him from feeling much anxiety about it.

The bishop had grown accustomed to the V, and able to stay on an even keel, but it took effort, and he knew that if he did not get the V out soon, he would likely succumb to the temptation to ditch reality again. It was too strong for him, the lure of such perfected unreality.

He had to wait for a launch because no one else was leaving the Bacchanal for New Baltimore. Demand for transportation from the solar system's largest party boat to the moon's only intentionally Catholic community was not high.

When a launch became available, he sat alone as it descended, feeling that he should be feeling something more. He was, after a lifetime on Mars, finally in Earth System, finally going to set foot in places he had heard about all his life. But the V prevented the expected emotional response.

It was such an important moment, he would have liked to be emotionally present for it.

The launch docked at the New Baltimore Port and the bishop sat unmoving. The gravity of the moon felt light after forty days on the Bacchanal.

"The moon," he thought. He had read about it so many times. He took a deep breath, stood up, and stepped out. He was surprised to find a crowd of well over a hundred gathered to greet him.

They were of all ages, including dozens of children. They gave a cheer when they saw the bishop. He noticed several people among them who appeared to be mentally disabled, including one of the children running and playing in a carpeted area to one side. There were also several women who were carrying children the natural way, in their own wombs.

One hardly ever saw such things on Mars.

A middle-aged man shook the bishop's hand, introduced himself as the mayor of New Baltimore, and welcomed the bishop on his first visit to Earth System.

It turned out there were more practicing Catholics in New Baltimore than on all of Mars, and it was a tradition among them to welcome any bishop who was making his first trip to Earth. The only reason there were not more of them was that the bishop's arrival happened to be in the middle of their night.

The mayor suggested that, if he was not too tired, the bishop might say a few words.

"I cannot tell you how grateful I am to be greeted so warmly," the bishop said. He told them that his trip had been much longer than he had expected, which drew a laugh, apparently because they had all followed the hijacking of the Frank Sinatra with great interest. He told them that, in all honesty, many of the things he had seen in his travels had left him wondering about the fate of humanity. There was so much irresponsibility and even evil in the world.

And then, feeling himself heading too much into dark themes, he told them about the faithful Catholics of Mars, and about how much he wished they could all come and meet so many wonderful brothers and sisters in the Faith.

There were refreshments, and the bishop shook many hands. Two priests, both young men, slim and fit, went out of their way to introduce themselves. They were the first members of the Cohort of the Church Militant that the bishop had ever met in person.

They were meticulously polite and addressed him not as "bishop" but in the old way as "Your Excellency."

The older of the two, Father Theo, was the more soft-spoken, and seemed to the bishop to be one of those holy souls one meets from time to time who draw attention to themselves by their disinterest in it.

The younger man, Father Augustus, struck the bishop as pious in the unattractive sense of the word, one of those characters who thinks knowing all the right answers in the catechism is the point of religious life.

Both men were dressed in the usual black coats and white collars of priestly life, but what they wore was far more elegant than was usual. White shirtsleeves with gold cufflinks poked out from their jacket sleeves. On their lapels they wore fine gold crucifixes, and their shoes were flawlessly polished.

They were in New Baltimore on their way out to the asteroid belt, where the Cohort ran schools and was reputed to hold considerable political sway.

"Will you be visiting Mars on your way out?" the bishop asked.

"Just the opposite." Father Theo smiled. "Our itinerary takes us in toward the sun for a gravity-whip out to the belt. We'll end up on the other side of the solar system from Mars, I'm afraid."

The bishop smiled at this, and was about to greet other guests when Father Augustus asked whether the bishop would welcome Cohort members on Mars.

An oddly pushy question from a young priest in an informal setting.

"We are mission territory," the bishop answered firmly. "Any good priest is welcome among us, so long as he is willing to take on the humble work of a missionary."

After an hour or so of visiting with the families of New Baltimore, the bishop was taken by the arm. "We do not want to wear you out in your first few hours with us," the mayor said. He walked the bishop to rooms that had been prepared for him at the Cathedral rectory.

The rooms were lovely, and the bishop was quickly off to sleep. In the morning he found a local parish priest and made a formal confession.

He then checked himself into the city's infirmary, where he was treated by a missionary doctor, who told him stories of her years caring for frontier families on Saturn's moon Titan. She kept him for two days of observation after removing the V and treating his depression.

On the night he was released, he joined New Baltimore Bishop Martino Pham and several governmental, academic, and spiritual leaders for a semi-formal dinner at the cathedral.

The bishop found he liked being among so many well-educated and enthusiastic Catholics. All his life he had lived in mission territory. Always he had been part of a tiny minority. And for the last month and a half he had been the sole practicing Catholic on a ship of hundreds of people.

Now he swam in a sea of Catholicism.

At dinner several people asked him if he had met Edgardo Leon. The bishop learned from them that Leon was responsible for the great ship now under construction in orbit above the moon. Leon had several patents that were key to high acceleration electric-plasma rocket motors. He was worth hundreds of billions, and he was spending most of his fortune on an interstellar project.

"Maybe Leon is right," a mother holding a two-year-old on her hip said as she wiped the child's face, "maybe we do need to start the whole world over again."

# (37.)

The bishop checked in with his missionary doctor the morning after the cathedral dinner. She told him that as long as he felt ready, she was ready to let him go on to Earth.

He did feel ready, though he also felt a bit overwhelmed at the thought.

"I grew up there," she told him, "so it is hard for me to imagine coming from Mars and seeing it for the first time. All I can tell you is that you will not be disappointed. I remember coming home from Saturn and, even though Earth is my home, it took me days to adjust to the beauty of it."

When he got back to his rooms at the rectory, the bishop found a conservatively dressed young man waiting with a handwritten note. The note was from Edgardo Leon, asking for the honor of the bishop's company at lunch.

"Of course," the bishop told the young man, "please tell Mr. Leon the honor is mine, and I would be happy to join him."

The young man asked for the bishop's blessing and, having knelt to receive it, he told the bishop that he would return a little after noon to take him to lunch.

The bishop found he enjoyed the formality of the messenger and the handwritten note. On one level, the whole thing was silly and very old-fashioned, of course. But on another, the precision of the manners spoke of a deep respect for persons. As much as all things pompous or artificial embarrassed the bishop, he was a sucker for manners. To have manners was to be humane.

Leon greeted the bishop at the door, showed him into a sitting room, and offered him a drink—which the bishop declined. The host was dressed stylishly— even if the style seemed somewhat formal and almost military in its precision. He was lean and tall, with waves of thick black and gray hair. His house was furnished in dark woods, tapestries, and brass.

The whole scene reminded the bishop of one of the adventure room melodramas back on the Bacchanal. He almost expected Leon to fight off a squad of assassins and become embroiled in a high-speed chase.

But Leon was a quiet, serious man with an affable smile. He thanked the bishop for coming, and congratulated him on his handling of the Frank Sinatra incident.

"I am not sure I did much," the bishop said honestly. "When you are kidnapped, a happy outcome is mostly up to the kidnapper."

"Well," Leon said, "Your kidnapper seems to be leading us all toward an unhappy outcome. May I ask your impression of him?"

The bishop was more than a little tired of this question, but something about Leon's manner eased whatever resentment he felt at having to repeat what he had already said so many times.

He told the story of his meetings with the Fuhrer in detail.

"Do you think he is in touch with reality?"

"I do," the bishop said. "He seems to truly believe in his philosophy."

"Ah. He is a visionary," Leon summed up. "Most people think that to be a visionary is a good thing, but it is almost always a bad thing. It almost always involves a grandiosity that works counter to the love of individuals."

"I have witnessed a great deal of grandiosity as I travelled here," the bishop said. "New Progressivism is no less grandiose, no less indifferent to individuals. It merely wraps its grandiosity and indifference in beautiful language about rights and progress."

Leon laughed. "What I would give for more bishops like you."

The bishop ignored the compliment. "I was told that you intend to start the world over," he said. "That sounds a bit grandiose."

Leon laughed again, but with resignation. "Do you think I might be another of these grandiose visionaries that so plague humanity?" he asked the bishop.

"I have no reason to think you are," the bishop said. "I just found the comment odd. What does it mean?"

"People say strange things," Leon shrugged. "But I must admit there is a kernel of truth in it. I have put a great deal of money into building an interstellar ship. It is designed travel to the Gliese star system. There is a planet there that appears to be at least as hospitable as Mars for human habitation, and probably quite a bit more. It is not a second Earth, but it has many very Earth-like qualities."

"You are sending people on this ship?"

"Certainly. At the speeds we will be able to attain in this new ship, it should take us about forty-three years to get there."

"You are going yourself?"

"I am, God willing, but it is not likely I will live to see the end of the journey."

"The people who return will be the third or fourth generation descendants of those who start the trip," the bishop said.

"No, you misunderstand," Leon answered. "We are going to colonize. We are not planning a return trip."

The bishop said nothing.

Leon continued. "The ship is called the Santa Maria. She can carry eighteen thousand souls, but we will leave with only about four and a half thousand. We should be near the full eighteen thousand by the time we arrive."

"You are starting over? That's what they mean when they say you are starting the world over?"

"Essentially, yes. Our colony is meant to be a Catholic colony. We will build a Catholic society."

"You will get away from all of the decadence and violence of this post-modern paradise we live in?"

"Yes."

"But is it really Catholic to run away from the world and its troubles?"

Leon did not seem at all flustered by this question, but shrugged and said, "If running away is what we were doing, then it would not be Catholic. The Holy Father made that very point to me. A Catholic must not turn his back on the world, but must be love in the midst of the world."

"And, yet, you are going."

"But we are not running away. We believe that the stars—at least those nearby—will sooner or later be colonized. Our idea is to colonize the very best nearby system—to claim it for God, if I may be so bold. Others will follow in time, but they will not find an empty place when they come. Instead, they will find a place built up and ready for them, with a culture and laws and a history grown from a Catholic root."

"A fascinating idea," the bishop said, and he meant it. What might such a world be like in a hundred years or so?

He and Leon discussed this question for a long while, the bishop pressing objections, Leon addressing each with a well-thought-out answer.

"You have thought of everything," the bishop teased him.

"No, bishop. That is impossible. But I have satisfied myself that this is worth doing."

"Then I am sure you have already considered," the bishop said at last, "the fact that the modern and post-modern worlds grew up from a Catholic root. It was in the Catholic medieval period that the roots of the modern world first sprouted, and the first shoots began to appear. There are no guarantees that ..."

"That we will produce good fruit?"

"Yes."

"That is not the point. We do not take on the mission because we are guaranteed of success. We are not idealists, and we have no utopian fantasies. We are going because we believe it serves the Lord. He will do with it what he wants."

"But isn't it a great risk? What are your chances of making it to your new planet alive?"

"My personal chances are near zero, but the mission's chances are actually quite high. Probes have already crossed to Alpha Centuri and Tau Ceti, as you know. Many other probes are in transit to other systems. It can be done. In fact, no interstellar ship has yet been lost, as far as we know. I am convinced we will make it."

"Not intending to be rude, but if it is so doable, why has no one else done it?"

"Other projects are planned, some have faltered, some are making slow progress. They are hard projects to finance, and I have an advantage in that area. Also, there are not many people willing to take the risk, to commit their lives, and their children's lives, and their grandchildren's lives to an adventure. Our people do not see it as an adventure, but as a vocation."

"And you will build settlements in the new system?"

"Yes, exactly as we now build settlements all around the solar system, even in difficult environments, such as Venus. Some people have called this, somewhat frivolously I am sure, the Second Ireland Project. Their way of explaining the project is to use Europe after the fall of Rome as an analogy. When Rome fell, Europe went illiterate. People used to call this the 'Dark Ages.' But in Ireland, far off the coast of Europe, hundreds of monasteries flourished. Monks and nuns went out to the edge of the known universe and built societies. Within these societies people remembered history. They remembered how to read. And at a certain point, when some Frankish king or other decided it was time for Europe to learn to read again, he called on the Irish monks to bring their knowledge to his kingdom."

"So you are going to preserve what is good because you believe a dark age is about to fall?"

"We are not prophets, but we believe the risks of such a turn are very high."

"I wish I could contradict that," the bishop said.

Leon leaned in and spoke animatedly, "A hundred years, or two hundred, or five hundred years from now, the civilization that we are going to build will be ready to serve all of humanity in much the way Ireland did for Europe. And we will do it merely by remaining Catholic and flourishing in a new place."

"Are you sure you are not running away?"

"Well, a tsunami is coming. We are running from that. We are running for high ground. And when the tsunami subsides, we will be ready to help the survivors."

"But it is not a tsunami. It is a human-made disaster. Why not stay and try to work against the disaster?"

"Many will stay. Millions and millions of Christians of every kind will stay. Only forty-five hundred are going. What we are doing is not evil, bishop. We are colonizing a new place. That is a noble cause in itself. We have the blessing of the Holy Father. He has even agreed to send us with bishops and priests."

"Please do not interpret my questions as condemnations," the bishop said quickly. "I suppose I just wanted to be sure you were not another nut. I have seen enough of nutty plans."

"I understand completely," Leon said graciously.

"To tell you the truth, I am very attracted to your idea," the bishop admitted. "I am convinced that this civilization is on a precipice. We have moved out into space, but without purpose. We are filling the emptiness with our emptiness. The UNAC, God love it, has tried to provide order, but it is what it has always been, a weak artifice. It is not a place or even an ideal; it is a wish. But even if it were not, no one can provide order in this vast solar system. All of the oldest evils— slavery, murder, tyranny—they have sprung up again. Qoheleth is right; there is nothing new under the sun."

"Or orbiting the sun!" Leon added.

"Right," the bishop laughed.

"We think alike on these things, bishop."

"Yes, but I am also bothered by your idea. I am not sure why, but it unsettles me almost as much as it appeals to me."

The two fell silent for a long moment. And then Leon spoke with deliberation.

"Dear bishop, your points are well taken. But I hope I will be able to overcome them. We need another bishop to come with us. Our search committee has asked me to ask you to consider it."

The bishop was stunned. He had a diocese to care for. He was grateful for the offer but ... He sputtered out a list of objections.

Leon did not bring it up again. He simply listened politely to the bishop's protests throughout the rest of the afternoon. By the time he left, the bishop had objected to the idea in every way he could think of.

But he had not said no.

# (38.)

The bus flight to Earth was nine hours. The bus orbited twice on its final approach. The bishop watched intently out the window, almost unable to believe that he had really come this far.

He had experienced Earth from space before; in fact, he had walked the streets of many Earth cities, but that was in pyramidal holograms or inside media lounges. To see the real Earth below him, its oceans and clouds and continents, was far more affecting than he had expected.

He found himself talking to God, prattling on, actually, about how beautiful it all was, pouring out thanks, and pointing to features of the planet as if God might have missed them.

The entry into the atmosphere was imperceptible but for the firing of the air-breathing engines. They made a crackling sound and a hum that was unlike any engine the bishop had ever heard. The descent took a solid hour, and the bishop had to turn away from the window every few minutes to work out the crick in his neck and the ache of the glare in his eyes.

In time, cities could be seen, and rivers. Then he saw, far out at sea, the Pacific Archipelago, the most extensive engineering project in human history, with living space for hundreds of millions of people in its billions of acres of surface and subsurface space.

The ocean was enormous, mile after mile of shimmering blue. The bus was on its final approach now, heading for the spaceport in New Mexico.

By the time it reached the coast of California, it was quite low, and as San Diego passed beneath, the bishop felt a rush of excitement that he truly was about to touch the Earth. He could make out buildings and a very old, curved bridge. Then came some low mountains followed by a wide farmland that seemed to go on for hundreds and hundreds of miles.

They passed more mountains—these seeming dangerously close—and then began a quiet final glide into port.

He could see vehicles now, and individual homes, and then people walking on the surface of the planet completely unprotected, wearing nothing but light clothing.

And then the Earth rushed up, the bus seemed to skim just above it for a breathless moment, and they were down, rolling along the space-port runway.

The bishop took out his beads and held the feet on the cross to his lips.

The bus rolled for a while and then turned to enter a hangar. The bishop could hardly get over the sight of the workers walking openly on the surface. The hangar doors did not close behind the bus, and yet the bus opened. The bishop had a moment of panic that the air would all just disappear.

Many of the travelers with him were obviously experienced at this. They grabbed their things and made their way out as quickly as they could. The bishop noticed that only a few remained in their seats, as if afraid to move.

First timers.

Of these, he was among the first to rise. He stepped down the steps and into the terminal.

Once in terminal, he headed directly for an outside door.

It was warm and dry here. He walked for a while almost uncomprehending.

He was walking on sand beside a building. There was light on the building. There was a road. The light was everywhere. Terror gripped him in waves, but he fought through it. He could survive outside here.

He had spent all of his life up to this moment in a container of one kind or another. Always there had been airlocks and radiation shielding and domes and walls and gel-glass between him and the harshness of nature. But now—out here—there was nothing to protect him from nature but nature itself. This atmosphere, this sky, and the magnetic layers that arced and bent above them were the only things that had kept and protected life for billions of years on this planet.

"Oh God, how frail it is, how untrustworthy it seems."

But Christ Himself walked under this sky— entrusted himself to its protection.

"I am on the very planet, the very Earth that His feet touched. I am breathing the air he breathed. And Abraham and Sarah, and Moses, and Elijah, and Micah, and John the Baptist, and all of them—Francis and Domenic, Katherine, Theresa. My God, they have all walked here, and now I am here, under your protecting sky, breathing your warm air."

As he looked up to the sky, terror swept over him again, but he fought it down.

And then he knelt, what else was there to do in the presence of so great a gift?

"No matter what anyone says about being a Martian or a Jovian or a station colonist or even a Cerean. This, this Earth, Lord, this is home."

# (39.)

He did not stay in New Mexico but took a tube over to Boston where there was a guesthouse for off-Earth clergy. For the first few days he was bothered by open windows and by the weird carelessness of the people here. They simply took for granted that the air would not whoosh away. It took him some time to feel comfortable with that.

And it took longer still to become comfortable with birds. The variety of flying creatures was astonishing; their calls and screeches and caws were omnipresent. Certainly, the bishop had seen birds before, but on Mars, birds remained an oddity kept to aviaries.

To see them everywhere completely free was frightening; they seemed so sinister. Local people hardly noticed them and seemed to find it entirely amusing how much they disturbed the bishop. He tried mightily to fit in and treat the little devils as if they were a normal part of life. But they distracted him, and kept him wondering where they might pop out and what they might try.

Squirrels bothered him, too. He was sure at any moment one would jump on him and send him into a complete panic.

He could hardly imagine ever getting used to living in such proximity to all this wildlife.

He had always thought of himself as a person who liked both animals and plants, but the plant life of Boston disturbed him almost as much as the wild birds and squirrels and insects. The plants were relentless and seemed to fit themselves into any available spot. Grass emerged from sidewalks and between bricks. Thin trees worked their way up through any odd spot of soil. Weeds, flowers, vines, and mosses took over even where there was no soil.

The air was filled with the smell of them, sometimes nearly overwhelming the bishop as he turned a corner or passed a particularly lush bloom.

He strained to imitate the locals in their almost total disregard of the wildness around them. He learned that birds on the ground would fly away if you just waded into them. He tried it, despite his better judgment, and though the birds did, indeed, scatter, he decided it would be best to simply walk around them in the future.

But when it came to the wildness of the sky, he simply could not comprehend the general nonchalance.

Very few people, if any, took notice of the sky. They seemed to take for granted its constantly changing nature, the coming and going of the sun and the moon, the passing of clouds—many types of clouds and colors. The bishop would find himself stopped in his tracks several times a day by some passing white giant or some swirl of baleful gray.

People would pass him as if nothing were happening at all. Nor did people attend much to the moisture of the air, which seemed to change by the hour. The atmosphere seemed as much a living thing as the creatures and the plants.

He felt now that he understood the pagan religions as he never could have had he stayed on Mars. The fearful livingness, the sense of many presences and many facets, gave life on the Earth an ominous and exhilarating spiritual feel.

It was all too marvelous and surprising, and was made all the more so by the fact that he seemed to be the only person noticing it.

The Maryknoll Fathers who staffed the guesthouse were patient with him, encouraging him to talk about how strange it all seemed, and helping him to deal with both his fears and his excitements. As the days went on, he found he was adjusting, though birds still seemed more menacing than the Earthlings were willing to admit.

The Nuncio contacted him after about a week to tell him that in ten days the pope would be able to see him. He was welcome to remain with the Maryknoll Fathers until then.

He passed the time by taking day trips on the tube to China, to Hawaii, and to several Latin American countries. It was in Buenos Aires that he found himself in a little chocolate shop and suddenly remembered the chocolates that he had been given on Ceres.

When he returned to his quarters at the guesthouse that evening, he opened the little bag, not really thinking about eating them—he still suspected they might be poisonous—but wanting merely to see whether they had survived the trip. If they had, he might have them scanned and, if free of poison, share them with the Maryknolls, who were jolly men, in general, and would probably get a kick out of eating some Cerean Fascist treats.

But when he opened the bag, the chocolates appeared to have been exploded from the inside.

He thought back on how the Cerean chocolatier had insisted he not eat them until he was on Earth, and he came to suspect that some kind of nano-constructors hidden within the chocolates had been set to activate once inside Earth's magnetosphere or when exposed to some other signature of Earth. Whatever the signal was, the nano-constructors had, indeed, activated, and now they had assembled themselves into a tiny metallic rectangle on which was written—something.

With effort, the bishop could just make it out, a 14-digit number: 07,873,393,200,302.

What the number meant, the bishop had no idea.

# (40.)

The bishop assumed the number meant something to someone, so he decided to memorize it and smash the metal piece, scattering bits of it around the planet as he continued his day trips.

Whatever it represented, he did not want it sitting around for someone to find.

If the number was valuable, the person who wanted it would have to explain what it was for.

That person presented herself when the bishop was on the tube back from visiting Eddie Cho's sister in Seoul, just a few nights before he was due to head to the Vatican.

"Bishop Gastelum," she said, offering her hand. She wore the uniform of a Fleet officer.

"Yes, have we met?" he said, extending his own hand and rising from his seat.

"No," she said sitting down across from him. "I am Lt. Commander Rasna Modi. I am here to retrieve something from you."

Sitting down again, the bishop said nothing. Instead, he offered her a quizzical look, as if to say, "What could I possibly have that would interest a Fleet officer?"

"I have a very good friend who is a chocolatier," Modi said. "He contacted me in a roundabout way and suggested he might have given you something."

"Ceres?" the bishop asked, deciding not to play games.

"Yes," Modi said, obviously pleased to be speaking frankly.

"Please tell me," the bishop asked, "does this have anything to do with David Elsman?"

"I cannot discuss David Elsman. There is no possible answer I can give that would be helpful in the current environment."

"Then perhaps we should continue our discussion in a more private environment," the bishop offered.

"That's not what I meant," Modi said. "I mean the diplomatic environment. The Fleet tries to maintain strategic ambiguity regarding all questions of spying. We simply do not answer such questions or discuss persons who may be suspected of spying."

"He was a spy," the bishop answered. "I have become sure of it. Why else would he have killed himself? He died for what he believed in, which was liberty—at least as the masses now define liberty. I am afraid we differed on that point, though I valued him as a bright and engaging friend."

The bishop immediately wished he had not used the term "the masses;" it sounded so political and old-fashioned.

"I did not know him," Modi answered without expression, but there was something about her lack of expression that was suggestive. She was holding back.

"The chocolates you are looking for did not survive my travels," the bishop said, satisfied that Modi had answered his questions about David Elsman. "Can you tell me why the Fleet might be interested in them?"

"Were they destroyed or does someone else have them?"

"Destroyed," the bishop answered. He was willing to honestly answer any question she had, except for one.

"Was there a number?"

He looked at her innocently. "Excuse me?"

Over the next half hour she asked about the number in numerous different ways. Each time, the bishop managed to be evasive, and in the end she changed the subject to his Vatican visit. She thought it must be a very important visit if he had come all the way from Mars. He explained the concept of the *Ad Limina* to her. She asked if she might pay him a visit again before he left Earth.

"Of course," he said, explaining the rest of his itinerary as far as he knew it.

As he left the tube station just outside of Boston and hailed a cab, he felt certain he had not been evasive enough.

Modi knew he had the number.

Further, he knew this conversation did not conclude the matter. Even now, she was probably reporting to some superior and strategizing about what moves to make next. As the cab rolled quietly through the streets of Cambridge and toward Boston, he found himself wondering whether the Fleet would resort to force to get information from him. After all, it had been valuable enough for both David and the chocolatier to risk their lives.

Perhaps they would, but they would not come to such a decision without trying other strategies first. Beating or torturing a Catholic bishop could be a public relations problem, if nothing else.

He felt certain she would make another friendly approach before any other methods were tried.

Strangely, the motives the bishop was currently having the greatest difficulty understanding were his own. Why did he not just give the number to the Fleet?

He told himself that he resisted doing so because he did not know what the number represented. These were dangerous times, lives were at stake, and the bishop could not be certain that delivering the fruits of espionage to the Fleet would help rather than hurt.

But could his anger at the Fleet, at the UNAC, at the madness and meanness of the whole New Progressivist worldview be clouding his judgment?

The Fascists were right about one thing: New Progressivism—with its mighty Fleet and its aura of UNAC legitimacy—was a corrupt and self-indulgent philosophy. It was adolescent in its constant reference to justice and peace as it imposed its will on others. It was adolescent in its constant need to create new grievances and then wed itself to those grievances, as if being aggrieved were the very height of nobility. It was adolescent in its demand for the comfort of conformity—asking everyone to think only the currently approved set of thoughts—while all the while pretending that New Progressivism was the only philosophy in the world that truly encouraged people to think for themselves. And it was adolescent in its ability to be blankly cruel—stupidly, insipidly, self-righteously cruel—while all the while insisting on its own enlightenment and gentility.

He had a right to be angry.

But none of that was the font from which the bishop's deepest anger flowed. From the time he was an altar boy in a Martian warren, he had been catechized to be aware of and cope with the idiocies of the New Progressivists.

No, his current anger—more than anger, his rage—was something he had been pushing down for weeks. Its name was Doug.

He didn't want to carry on an endless dialogue with a society that could allow such things to be done every day to perfectly innocent people. He wanted to end it.

He was not sure he wanted to help them defeat the Fascists. Maybe a purifying fire was just what was needed.

# (41.)

Before going to the Vatican, the bishop packed his things, thanked the Maryknoll fathers, and took the tube to Jerusalem. He found he could not read or pray as he passed beneath the Atlantic Ocean on his way to the holy city. Outside its walls, the living God had hung upon a Roman cross. There were missionary sisters on the moons of Saturn today carrying the news of it. How many billions of people had carried the news of it? In how many places?

He stayed two days in Jerusalem. He visited Bethlehem and the Sea of Galilee. He wended his way through the narrow streets of the Old City, replete with living memory of Christ and those who had come before Him.

He hardly spoke with anyone the whole time. What words could express it? Silence was best.

A bishop of Mars had come to the land of Abraham, Isaac, and Jacob. And soon he might well be the first bishop to travel to another star.

He felt deeply meditative and found himself caressing the cross that hung from his beads when at last he made the trip beneath the Mediterranean on his way to Rome.

He could not go directly to the Eternal City, however. Rome had no tube station under it. Instead, the Romans had built a station under the ancient port of Ostia.

A quaint, old monorail took him the last thirty kilometers from Ostia to Rome. It was slow, and it made several stops en route, which meant the trip took almost half an hour.

Before the monorail had left its first station, however, the bishop found himself with a traveling companion. Lt. Commander Rasna Modi sat down next to him and asked politely if she could have a few moments of his time.

"Of course," the bishop said.

"I have come to level with you, and to ask you for your help. I think when you hear what the numbers you are carrying in your head represent, you will want to help me."

The bishop did not think so, but he was willing to listen.

"On his visit to Ceres, your friend David Elsman came into possession of some very valuable information. When he killed himself, he was carrying in his head the same numbers you are now carrying. He knew what was in store if the Fascists got their hands on him. They would have tortured him and confused him, and he would have talked. He would have endangered a great many people.

"The information, as I am sure you have already guessed, is encoded. In themselves, the fourteen digits you have are worthless. But when decoded, they will tell us the location of an asteroid that we very much need to find. Within the core of this asteroid, the Fuhrer is building an attack fleet.

"Our understanding of the Fuhrer's plan is limited. I must be honest with you on this point. But all our psychological profiles suggest he is likely preparing a lightning strike that will allow him to reach his strategic goals without a prolonged war. It is likely that his ultimate goal is control of Earth System. If we can prevent this, millions, perhaps billions, of lives may be saved. We have no certainty of winning even if we can defeat his first strike and draw him into a protracted war, but it is at least better than a quick defeat.

"Bishop, I know that you are not entirely sympathetic to New Progressivism, but I cannot imagine that you have any sympathies for the Fascists. Do you want the world as we know it to be ripped apart?"

This was serious, indeed. But, in truth, he was not sure how to answer her question.

He felt cold to her entreaties. And he answered her coldly before stepping off the monorail into the heart of Rome.

"I'm sorry, Lt. Commander; I cannot help you."

# (42.)

The bishop's comcom led him several blocks from the monorail station into a labyrinth of tight cobblestone streets. Along one of these, a hillside street with a severe slope, the comcom stopped him in front of a four-story building.

Its square windows and yellow stucco façade looked as if they could have survived from the ancient Roman world, though the building had only stood a century or two on this spot. It had once been a boutique hotel.

An eight-foot hedge surrounded the building, now owned by Carmelites who ran it as a guesthouse for off-Earth clergy.

The bishop lifted the latch on an old iron gate set into the hedge, stepped in, and gently latched it again behind him.

It was quiet within the shrubbery wall. He felt an immediate sense of calm.

The front door was glass. A Carmelite brother in his dark brown tunic and cowl got up from his desk when he saw the bishop approach.

"Mark Gastelum," the bishop said when the brother opened the door.

"Yes, welcome, bishop," the brother said as he let the bishop in and stepped toward the porter's desk. "I am Brother Stephen," he said.

The lobby was very basic, with tile floor, wooden beamed ceiling, and a handmade sign on the desk that said, "Please ring for the porter." Beside the sign was a wooden-handled brass bell.

Other than the desk and a few wooden chairs, the lobby was empty.

The plainness of the surroundings seemed entirely calculated to draw the eye to a great golden image of Christ the Pantocrator that covered the back wall.

"It is magnificent," the bishop said as he surveyed the image.

Brother Stephen smiled and nodded.

The bishop found the Carmelites less jovial than the Maryknolls of Boston, but in their quiet way, exceptionally hospitable. They swept the floors with brooms, bowed slightly when they greeted a guest, and moved slowly.

Time seemed plentiful, and the brothers seemed to spend it lavishly on small tasks.

The bishop followed Brother Stephen up one flight of stairs.

"Your room," Brother Stephen said, stopping at a room as simple as the lobby, with wooden furniture and tile floors. What appeared to be a hand-painted copy of Rubelev's *Icon of the Trinity* was the only decoration.

When Brother Stephen had left, the bishop unpacked his things and placed them in the wooden drawers of a hutch. He folded his clothes precisely and in silence, unwilling to disturb the slow and quiet spirit of the house. He sat in the room's only chair and read until his comcom told him it was time to go down to dinner.

The dining room was by no means full. Around one end of a big wooden table that could easily have seated fourteen guests sat three Carmelite brothers and two visiting priests. A fourth brother, a white apron wrapped around his tunic, served the table. Everyone stood when the bishop entered.

Brother Stephen made introductions. Brother Alphonsus, in the apron, was the house cook and provisioner, and Brothers Thomas and Bede maintained the house and grounds.

Father Emmanuel Charles, a compact and slightly round man with unkempt white hair and bushy eyebrows, was a missionary to the mid-atmosphere colonies of Venus.

And Monsignor William Ryan, a tall, square-shouldered man in his sixties with the meaty hands of a former athlete, was an administrator from the University of Notre Dame's asteroid belt campus.

All greeted the bishop cordially and waited for him to sit before retaking their seats.

Dinner began with cheese, bread, and vegetable soup. Then came gnocchi with red sauce. Wine was poured from carafes on the table, and dessert was strawberries with sweetened cream. The brothers were generally reserved, but the three priests carried on a cheerful banter throughout the meal.

There was very little mention of politics, which the bishop appreciated, but a great deal of comedy about the various adventures each had had as space travelers. The bishop told the story of this departure from Mars in a scramjet with particular relish, and drew laughs even from the brothers when he told about his near certainty of death as the craft plummeted.

All had settled down to enjoying their strawberries, and Msgr. Ryan was explaining the anxiety that was growing among students about the possibility of war, when the porter's bell rang.

"Excuse me," Brother Stephen said as he stood up to answer the bell, "I forgot to mention that we have a late-arriving guest this evening."

The Carmelites did not use robots, so Brother Bede accompanied Brother Stephen in case there were bags to handle.

In a moment, Brother Stephen returned with the late-arriving guest.

The bishop recognized him instantly: Father Augustus, as slim, flawlessly dressed, and cordial as ever.

"Please do not rise on my account," he said. "I am intruding on your dinner. I will just slip in and join you, if I may."

Brother Alphonsus quickly set a place across from the bishop for Father Augustus and set out bread, cheese, and soup.

"Your plans changed," the bishop said.

"Indeed they did, and rather suddenly," Father Augustus rolled his eyes and shrugged. "I have been recalled to Earth temporarily to help settle an issue for the order."

"You two have met?" Msgr. Ryan asked. The bishop was not certain if he heard an accusation implied in the question.

"Just recently," the bishop answered. "I was in New Baltimore preparing to come to Earth while Father was preparing for a trip to the asteroid belt."

"But the Cohort needed you on Earth?" Msgr. Ryan asked.

"Yes, monsignor. I am officially a secretary of the order, but I function, on occasion, as a kind of ambassador when the Cohort comes up against a touchy situation."

"You solve problems," Msgr. Ryan said.

"In general, yes."

Father Augustus seemed entirely comfortable, treating Msgr. Ryan's questions as friendly, though it seemed to the bishop that they were anything but.

"I live in the asteroid belt," Msgr. Ryan said. "And I have had occasion to deal with the Cohort of the Church Militant on several occasions. It seems that troubles follow your order."

"Indeed they do," Father Augustus answered agreeably. "We have made it our mission to defend the Church in places that others avoid. That tends to bring trouble."

"I think you are the first member of the Cohort that I have ever met," Father Charles interrupted. "All I ever hear about your group is that you are Fascists. To me, that seems an awfully uncharitable thing to say."

"Thank you, Father, for saying so," Father Augustus said. "I would not like to be thought a Fascist."

"But your order does maintain close relations with Ceres," Msgr. Ryan challenged.

"We do, yes, and I suppose it is fair to expect some guilt by association. But you must remember that there are a great many Catholics among the Fascists. We try to minister to them. And we try to temper the violent streak within Fascism."

"But do you challenge the Fascists?" Msgr. Ryan pressed. "We must not shrink from speaking clearly about the murderous actions of this Fascist regime."

"Nor about the murderous actions of the New Progressivists," Father Augustus answered, still in an entirely friendly tone.

"Bishop," he said, "you have seen a bit of the New Progressivist world in your travels. Wouldn't you agree with me that its violence and cruelty—though they come cloaked in language about dignity and humanity—are deserving of the Church's condemnation?"

The bishop allowed himself a long breath before answering. "If we give people what they deserve, we are not much of a Church," he said. "Though I have to admit to great disappointment with what I have seen in my recent travels. I do not see much hope for either Fascism or New Progressivism."

A polite silence followed the bishop's comments, and a pursing of lips. The bishop found he sometimes got this respectful quiet. People expected wisdom from bishops, and it seemed to create awkwardness when what bishops had to say turned out to be a disappointment.

# (43.)

Bishop Nwame Abayo was a tall man with a rumbling, good-humored voice. The night before the Bishop of Mars was to meet with the pope, Bishop Abayo welcomed him to Rome and introduced him to several curial officials.

In the morning, the Bishop of Mars met at the Vatican with the Congregation for Education, the Mission Congregation, and several other departments to share information about the life of the Church on Mars and to receive input from the Holy See that he could take back to his diocese.

For the most part, the bishops he met were not at all what he had expected, though he was not really sure what he had expected. For one thing, he was surprised at how much deference they gave him as the spiritual leader of a whole planet, even if the population of the entire planet was less than that of the City of Rome.

Now, as he sat just outside the pope's office, Bishop Abayo teased him. "Everyone has said at some time, 'If I were advising the pope, I would tell him this or I would suggest that.' Well, now is your chance. Do you know what advice you are going to give the Holy Father?"

"I suppose I will be getting more advice than I will be giving," the Bishop of Mars answered.

Abayo chuckled at this. "That may be true; that may be true," he said. "But I have known the Holy Father for a very long time. Perhaps you did not know this, but he ordained me a priest when he was Bishop of Abuja. I have been his secretary here for nearly a decade. And I know he will be very open to hearing from you. You are an important bishop from one of the solar system's most important mission territories."

"I have never thought of myself as an important bishop."

"That is probably healthy." Abayo chuckled. "But do you think the Holy Father takes every bishop's calls? There are almost 11,000 bishops in the solar system."

"I don't understand," the bishop said. "I cannot remember ever having called him."

Abayo seemed to find this intensely amusing. "Who do you think answered you when you sent a message from the station—what was its name—the Merton Station?"

"Melton Station," the bishop said. "The Holy Father was the one who answered me?"

"Who else can send a message under papal seal?" Abayo asked, his eyes wide with playful astonishment.

"I thought it must be the Secretary of State of the Prefect of the Congregation for the—" The bishop stopped because Abayo was laughing out loud now.

"Dear Bishop Gastelum, you are mistaken," he said with obvious affection. "I received your message. I shared it with the Holy Father, and he responded immediately."

It took a moment to process what Abayo was saying. He thought of Ovca. How had the Holy Father known?

"Why did the Holy Father command me to preach to the leaders of the Melton Station?" he asked quietly. "Did he have some kind of information about the situation?"

Bishop Abayo did not laugh at this, but looked genuinely perplexed.

"I do not have access to all of the information the Holy Father has," he said. "But until your message, I don't think he knew anything about the Melton Station."

"But he commanded me to preach to the leaders of the station."

Now Abayo's laughing manner returned. "If you will forgive me for saying the obvious, you are a bishop. Souls were in grave danger. He sent you to be a shepherd."

It took a moment, but the bishop accepted this answer. And he began to see a strange effect of his having been raised a Catholic on Mars. Some part of him had thought of the clergy from Earth—and especially at the Vatican—as different from himself. Without realizing that he was thinking it, he had assumed that he was backward by their standards, that they would have answers and insights that he lacked—even, perhaps, access to secrets that shaped their decision.

He expected them to be company men, but found them to be more like parish priests. Why had it never occurred to him that that is just what they were? All of them had set out to be parish priests. Most of them had been – just like him, and then a call had come from the nuncio asking them to be bishops.

They had huge responsibilities now, sure, but the manner of their faith was nothing different than might be found in any parish on Mars.

He found this intensely comforting. There was no hidden center of the Church. It was all there in public, and even the least educated miner from the smallest moon of Saturn could grasp its main points and live them.

Abayo was good company, and the bishop enjoyed several more minutes of pleasant conversation with him before word came that the pope was ready. The bishop stood up, surprised at how nervous he suddenly became.

Abayo said, "We Nigerians are very friendly. I think you will enjoy your time with the Holy Father."

"Thank you," the bishop answered just as the pope's door opened.

There were three great windows in the pope's office and through them the bishop could see the dome of St. Peter's. The office was large and filled with light; its walls were covered in art. On the floor was an intricately woven rug that could have been brand new or, just as easily, hundreds of years old. There were bookshelves behind the pope's desk; there was also a sitting area with couches and chairs in the middle of the room.

And there at the door was a small and rather frail-looking old man in a white cassock. His skin was no longer its formerly deep, rich brown, and his hair and beard were almost entirely white.

Pope Clement.

"Bishop Gastelum," he said, holding out his arms in welcome.

"Holy Father," the bishop said, stepping uncertainly forward.

The pope embraced the bishop and kissed him on the cheek. "Welcome, my brother in Christ. I understand it has been a long and difficult journey."

# (44.)

The Fuhrer had been wrong in his Latin translation. *Ad limina* did not mean "to the light." That would be *ad lumena* or *ad lucem.*

*Ad limina* meant "to the thresholds."

When a bishop came to Rome for his required visit, he came as a pilgrim to the thresholds of the tombs of the Apostles Peter and Paul. The day after his meeting with Pope Clement, the bishop descended the stairs beneath the altar at St. Peter's Basilica to visit the burial place of the first of the Apostles, Peter himself.

The site upon which the great basilica now sat had once been a street of tombs, and tradition that dated back to imperial times held that, after his execution under the Roman emperor Nero, Peter had been interred here. Around the year 330, the Emperor Constantine had the whole area covered in dirt so that a church could be built on the site. The entire church was oriented so that one particular tomb would rest just beneath the altar.

That tomb had lain undisturbed under the altar of Constantine's church and then under the altar of its successor—the current Basilica of St. Peter—until sometime in the 1900s, when archeologists began to dig in the area. They discovered scores of ancient tombs, and one, the one under the altar, that may well have been the tomb of Peter himself.

It bore a Greek inscription that was badly damaged and could be read one of two ways: "Peter is here" or "Peter is not here."

The bishop loved this fact. As in all things, the Lord left room for the individual heart to decide.

The smell of earth was heavy as he descended. The air was moist. For him, a man of Mars, the enclosed space was, in some ways, far more comfortable than the vast open church above. He walked along a street about a hundred meters long. On each side of the street were tombs.

Halfway down the street, a pyramidal projector had been installed. When he stepped into it, the world was transformed. He was standing in Imperial Rome.

Instead of a church above his head, there was sky and, to one side, the old Vatican Hill. All around him were the same tombs, but they were brand new. The earliest Christians, perhaps Peter himself, had celebrated the Eucharist here—repeating the words of Christ, reading from the Scriptures, and singing hymns. They celebrated among the tombs for safety, and, perhaps, because it fit with their expectation that the dead would soon rise.

The bishop surveyed ancient Rome for a few moments. It was not so different from the world he inhabited, a fact that made him feel close to Peter.

The bishop stepped through the pyramidal projector and was again beneath the church among the ruins of the world he had just seen resurrected by technology.

Ahead of him was the tomb.

In his own lifetime, Peter had laid his hands upon men to give them the apostolic power that had been given to him by Jesus. One of these—a man named Linus—had led the Roman Christians in their mourning for the loss of both Paul and Peter at the hands of Roman executioners. In that year, hundreds of other Christians had been burned and crushed and torn apart during Nero's persecution.

And that man Linus—that first successor of Peter and Paul to lead the Church after their deaths—had laid his hands upon a successor. And that same laying on of hands had gone on in an unbroken line from the Apostles even to a young warren priest of Mars.

"I have come a long way to say thank you," the bishop said to the tomb. "I have come to ask for your prayers so that I may persevere."

The bishop was not a man who heard voices or saw visions or was given great signs. But he was a man of faith, and his faith made the short time he spent at Peter's tomb, though it was outwardly quiet and uneventful, a revelation.

He sat quietly on the steps of the tomb and meditated with Peter.

Images from Peter's life and from his own mixed with one another, but in no obvious order. It was not as if a story was being told, but as if memories from two minds were occurring at once, arising from the unknown depths to flit across the bishop's consciousness, where they would trigger more memories and dislodge more from the depths that would come rising up.

He thought a great deal about the first time Peter—then called Simon—had seen Jesus. And he thought about the times that Peter and Jesus would be alone. And he thought about Peter watching Jesus care for the poor. And the way Jesus could not fit into Peter's world of power and status and the insularity of family and clan and nation, so that Peter had had to leave his world and enter the one that Jesus proposed.

"See, Peter, I am making all things new," Jesus had said.

And the bishop answered, "Yes, Lord, I see."

This new world was a world in which God is love, and love is eternal—a world not of power and status and insularity, but of forgiveness and meekness and love without limits.

Peter had come to live in the new world proposed by Christ, and there was no way to live in it and also live in the Roman world without suffering.

So Peter had suffered.

The bishop saw his suffering: the beatings, the ridicule, and finally the crucifixion outside of Rome, the utter expulsion from the heart of the world.

And then the bishop knew that he was not going with Edgardo Leon to settle around a new star. It was a noble undertaking, but he was the Bishop of Mars, and he was going home to suffer with his people.

War was coming, and if there was to be a fire reigned down by the Fascists, he was going to resist it, to undermine it wherever he could, and his tool was going to be love.

"What a fool I have been," he said to Peter's tomb, and it almost seemed as if the tomb itself would laugh. The bishop remembered a rooster crowing.

"We have all been fools," the bishop said. "But we have been called to live in a new world where fools are welcome and their failings are all forgiven so long as they will love."

He sat a long time with Peter and shared memories.

He told the fisherman that he had decided to give the numbers to Modi. It had been anger that kept him from doing it up to now. He did not need that anger anymore.

When he came up, again, to the basilica, the tall and jovial Bishop Nwame Abayo was waiting for him.

"They grew concerned that you might have fallen asleep, so they sent for me," he said, laughing.

The Bishop of Mars smiled meekly.

"So you have gone to the threshold," Abayo said.

"Yes, and now I know my vocation."

Abayo laughed loudly at that, his most jovial laugh. "God is good," he said as he put a great arm around the bishop's shoulders.

"Amen," the Bishop of Mars said, laughing now just as heartily as the pope's secretary.

Abayo began singing a joyful hymn, and the two of them sang it together as they walked down the aisle of the great church. To some who saw them, it seemed that a pair of bishops had had too much to drink.

# (45.)

The bishop did not ask his comcom to tell him how to get back to the Carmelite guesthouse. He was in no hurry, and he was fairly certain he remembered the way.

He stopped into a bookshop and on a whim bought a leather-bound copy of *The Way of Perfection* as a gift for Brother Stephen to put into the house library. The Carmelites still read physical books and kept a large room full of them.

As he continued his stroll, he watched a painter try to capture the spirit of an ancient staircase, and then he listened by a fountain as two singers gave a lovely rendition of *Au Fond du Temple Saint.* The gathered crowd showed its appreciation with hearty applause and with coins and bills dropped into a hat.

Up and down the twisting streets the bishop walked and breathed in Rome, hoping to remember the smells once back on Mars.

At the iron gate of the Carmelite house, he got the idea that there should be a guesthouse for visiting clergy on Mars. He would ask Brother Stephen about it.

He let the gate close behind him and stood looking at the house for a moment before going in.

*Pacem in terris*, he thought to himself. It was a prayer, certainly, but it was also the plain truth. There was peace on Earth. It sang from the place, if only people would listen.

He felt the peace, tonight, and so felt the great sadness of its lack.

As he neared the house, he could see through the glass of the front door. Brother Stephen lay dead in a great pool of blood, a gaping wound in his neck. A woman was crouched over him and seemed to be searching his body for something. When she turned and saw the bishop at the door, his shock was complete.

Modi.

She stood and stepped toward him.

He ran, expecting to feel a hot lance in his back as he unlatched the gate.

Instead he heard her voice at the door behind him.

"Bishop, stop."

The lance never came, and he slipped out the gate, running along the hedge and down the street.

A car pulled out in front of him at the cross street. They were going to kill him here, he was certain, or grab him for torture.

He heard Modi at the gate behind him. The car door swung open and Father Augustus waved him in.

"Bishop, stop," Modi yelled. The light of a lance missed him by no more than a foot or two, striking the car.

He nearly dove in, and at a command from Father Augustus, the car sped away.

"Are you hurt?" Father Augustus asked.

"They killed Brother Stephen!"

"They. . .? Yes, that is why I was running," Father Augustus replied.

"Go to the Vatican," the bishop said. "They have security."

"I'm afraid we can't do that. Vatican security has been compromised. Modi intends to take you, and she will call on her plants at the Vatican to help. The Cohort has a house here in Rome. It is very secure."

"Fine." The bishop turned to look out the back of the car. No one seemed to be following.

"Bishop, I must be honest with you," Father Augustus said.

"What?—I am sorry, Father, what is it you are saying?"

"You are in shock, bishop, but I must speak with you."

The bishop was uncertain. Was he in shock? He was confused. He was angry. He just wanted it to be quiet so that he could decipher what was happening.

"I have cost Brother Stephen his life," he said aloud.

"That is what I want to speak with you about."

"What is it, Father?" The annoyance was clear in the bishop's voice.

"They believe you are carrying information. That is why I was sent back here. The Cohort got word that you might be a target. The information you have is very valuable. They will torture and kill for it. Do you know what information I am talking about?"

"Why did they kill Brother Stephen?"

"They were searching the place, he came upon them. I saw it and ran. They must have killed him because of something he saw. Maybe they thought he had it on him."

"What? What could he have had on him?"

"The information you are carrying. They must have thought—"

"Why would he have it? None of this makes sense."

As the bishop said this, a lance hit the car. It was not a hand lance, but something big, perhaps fired from a building or a truck.

A sick, burning smell erupted and the car spun out of control. The entire back end of the vehicle was gone. The seat wrapped itself around the bishop just as what remained of the car slammed into a wall. There was a loud crunch as the car hit, but the seat protected the bishop from harm.

"Are you injured?" the car asked.

"No," the bishop responded. Slowly the seat retracted its cocooning mechanisms and released him.

He struggled his way out of the mangled car.

Modi was there, half a block away; she was strapped into a flight pack and advancing in a shooting stance with a hand lance pointed at him.

Everything went strangely quiet and clear. A swarm of insect-like police bots formed, lighting up the crash scene.

The bishop felt he might be sick.

"Stop," Modi yelled. "I will shoot."

*Why is she yelling? I am not moving.*

The lights from the police bots were too bright.

"Stop," Modi yelled again very loudly, and almost in the same instant she fired her lance.

Something heavy slammed into the back of the bishop's legs, and he felt a sharp pain in his left calf.

It took him a moment to figure out what had happened, and Modi was standing beside him by the time he understood that he had been stabbed.

"He was crawling over the car," Modi explained as the bishop surveyed the body of Father Augustus slumped at his feet, a lance burn in his chest.

"He stabbed me," the bishop said.

Too much adrenaline. The world spun and went black. He did not even feel himself hit the ground.

# (46.)

The bishop awoke in an ambulance, but for a moment he did not open his eyes. He lay still and breathed in and out, taking time to recover as a mask over his face gave him oxygen.

He was alive, but Brother Stephen was dead. He prayed a prayer of sorrow and of thanks.

He struggled for a moment to understand why Brother Stephen was killed.

He opened his eyes. Modi was there, sitting silently beside his right shoulder while a small, metallic medic worked on his leg.

Modi smiled at him.

He lifted his right hand, pointed his index finger into the air, and wrote out a series of numbers.

"These are real?" she asked.

The bishop nodded and closed his eyes.

She relayed the numbers to someone over her comcom.

That done, she patted the bishop's shoulder and said, "Thank you."

He shrugged weakly at her and then closed his eyes to rest.

But he needed an answer. He pulled the mask away from this face. "Why did they kill Stephen?"

"He walked in on Father Augustus planting surveillance equipment," Modi said, still patting his shoulder. "I saw it on the equipment we had planted, but I could not get there in time."

"Why was Father Augustus planting surveillance equipment?"

"He is a Fascist collaborator, as far as we can tell. He meant to find out what information you had, and failing that, he meant to kill you."

"And if he had, you would have been left vulnerable to the Fuhrer's surprise attack."

"Yes."

The bishop thought quietly for a moment before saying, "I thought you were shooting at me."

"You had what I needed, bishop. I've been trying to keep you alive and well."

# (47.)

ROME -- The Catholic Bishop of Mars is in the news yet again, this time because of a bizarre car chase through the streets of Rome that left a priest dead and the bishop badly wounded.

Martian Bishop Mark Gastelum appears to have been kidnapped after visiting with Pope Clement XVII. The kidnapper, Father Augustus Reiser, was a member of the controversial Cohort of the Church Militant, and it is not yet clear what his motives were.

The bishop was under Fleet surveillance at the time of the kidnapping, "regarding possible threats against the bishop from foreign powers," according to a Fleet spokesperson. A Fleet satellite lance was fired at the kidnapper's moving car, disabling it and sending it careening into the side of a supermarket.

Following the crash, the bishop attempted to flee and was stabbed in the leg by his kidnapper, who was then fatally lanced by an unidentified Fleet Intelligence officer.

Pope Clement was informed of the incident before retiring for the evening, according to the Vatican Press Office, which added that the pope, "Was deeply disturbed at this violence, especially involving a priest. The Holy Father offers his prayers for Bishop Gastelum's recovery and for the soul of Father Augustus."

This is the second kidnapping for Bishop Gastelum in less than a year...

# (48.)

Modi sounded surprised to get the call, but she agreed to meet the bishop for dinner at a popular restaurant just outside the Vatican's walls.

"Lt. Commander Modi, I owe you an apology," he said as they waited for the hostess to secure them a table.

Modi looked at him closely. She was an intelligence agent, and it was her job to understand the situation, the context. At least that is how the bishop interpreted her study of him.

"I thought you were going to get on that ship out of the solar system and leave us all here to burn," Modi said.

"You knew about that?"

"You had to know we've been keeping an eye on you."

"Yes. I suppose I did," the bishop answered. "But no, I am not leaving the solar system. I am going home to Mars."

"I don't understand you," she said just as the hostess returned to seat them.

After both of them had ordered, they chatted innocuously for a while.

It turned out Modi was married and had a daughter. She showed the bishop pictures and exuded pride as she spoke about her daughter's skill as a hockey player.

As they got to know one another, the bishop regretted deeply that he had been so cold.

The waiter delivered their drinks, two tall beers. The bishop found he really liked the variety of beers available on Earth. He raised his glass to toast Modi's health and then drank deeply.

He let the beer settle in, gripped the sides of the small table, and leaned in toward Modi.

"Part of me wanted the world to be punished for all its wickedness. I wanted it to be slapped in the face so that it would repent."

"I gathered that," Modi said. "My sense is that you are not happy with all the changes that our world has brought, all the freedom to—"

"We Christians built a world in which the modern idea of freedom became possible," he interrupted her. "The only freedom I am opposed to is the kind that assaults the dignity of the human being."

"But who decides what is dignified?"

"We do not decide what is dignified. We discover it."

"I'm afraid I'm not very good at philosophy," Modi shrugged.

The bishop paused and drank more beer. "Every generation, every person, has to discover it anew," he said quietly, more to himself than to Modi. "I decided to help you because even a sick freedom is better than the slavery of Fascism. Even a world that is destroying itself in fantasy and pride is filled with people hungry for reality and ready to accept it humbly."

The waiter set their plates down in front of them.

"Bishop, do you really believe we are destroying ourselves?"

"I do."

"But you are going to stay with us anyway."

"There is always hope, so long as there are people who can respond to God when he calls."

"People like Father Augustus?"

"Now, Rasna, that is unfair, don't you think?"

"But he believed in Christ just as you do, bishop. Don't you agree with him that the Church possesses the truth?"

"Yes, I do. But the truth must be chosen, never imposed. He seemed to think he could impose the Church if he hooked it to the power of the Fascists."

"That's funny," Modi said. "I suppose that is what I feel about New Progressivism. It does not impose itself on anyone. People can do what they choose. Perhaps we agree on that. People must be free to choose."

"Yes. And that is an important agreement. It is one we do not share with the Fascists."

"So why are you so against us?"

"I am not against you. I think you are wrong about something. There is an important detail that you have overlooked. This great, innovative world you are building is not really very committed to freedom. New Progressivism imposes on others every time it allows a person to be cloned, or a fetal person to be killed, or—"

"Oh, OK. I see where you are going. Are you saying we are all totalitarians?"

"We are all sinners."

"Well, then, there is no hope. If we are all sinners, then we are just lost, aren't we? We will always think we are doing good no matter what evil we do."

"Well, unless someone comes who is not a sinner. Someone who knows the way and can teach us with authority."

Modi smiled at this. "You are trying to convert me, bishop."

"I'm trying to offer you a choice."

Modi smiled again and drank deeply. "You know, I am not a believer."

She placed the glass back down. "But I like the idea of talking about sin. I wonder if it is possible to think of sin in purely secular terms. Sometimes we do wrong, and we do it for no other reason than we want to. I see a lot of that."

"I see a lot of that, too," the bishop said, "when people come to ask forgiveness for what they have done. It might be that you could have a secular idea of sin, but forgiveness is divine, and we need it like we need water."

Modi didn't really seem to know what to make of that, so she changed the subject.

"We don't know how the Cohort got word that you might be carrying information," she told the bishop. "It seems most likely that they have infiltrated our intelligence office."

"That doesn't sound good."

Modi made a face at the obviousness of the remark. "No, it's not."

"Can I assist in any way?"

"I don't think so. Vatican security is helping us. They do not seem to believe that the Cohort is all rotten, but they have accepted that is has some bad members."

"I should hope so! They tried to kill me."

"Well, to be fair, that was only after their other plans didn't work out."

"So my fate was to be torture instead of just murder."

"Yes, but once Father Augustus saw that he was not going to get you secured away, he decided just to kill you."

"And that is when you saved me with your marksmanship."

"I'm not a marksman. That was a lucky shot."

The bishop thought about this for a moment, but could come up with no light-hearted riposte. "Thank you for what you did, Rasna."

"You are very welcome, Bishop."

They ate in silence for a moment and then Modi said, "May I ask a somewhat brazen question?"

"OK."

"What do you talk about when you meet with a pope?"

"Well, I've only met with one. But he wanted to know a lot about Mars. He wanted to know about what's going on out there in the asteroid belt, on Ceres, on the station colonies. He asked me to form a committee to begin working on a coordinated plan for missions to what he calls the 'wild areas.'"

"All business, then?"

"Yes, I suppose." The bishop laughed. "In fact, just before I left him he told me never to forget what business we are in. He said we only have one item to sell."

"Did you know what he meant?"

"Of course I did," the bishop chuckled as he twirled his spaghetti.

# (49.)

The Fuhrer had not swept down on Earth like a purifying fire. A Fleet contingent had been waiting to keep the vanguard from its rendezvous with glory.

Modi had been right; what followed was long and ugly: a war that reached into every part of the system. Entire colonies exploded, burned, and died in the silence of space.

Forty-five-hundred Catholics escaped: a seed pod carried on the wind before the blaze.

And Mars was cut off.

The Fleet created a zone of protection around both Earth and Mars. But travel between them became impossible. Even communication became spotty. Refugees from station colonies poured into Mars by the hundreds of thousands. Many had left everything behind as they fled the Fascist onslaught.

Food became scarce at times, but virtually every decorative plant on the planet was uprooted to be replaced with grains or vegetables. Somehow, everyone was fed.

The bishop organized relief efforts, and temporary housing, and hospital facilities, all with the help of his small but growing flock. The spirit of cooperation on Mars became infections. Everyone pitched in either in defense of the planet or in seeing to the needs of the refugees.

With Eddie's help, Doug completed his preparation and received the sacraments from the bishop at Prince of Peace Abbey.

The abbey had become an enormous hospital, and Eddie spent most of every day visiting the sick, changing bandages, helping patients with rehab, or feeding them when they could not feed themselves. Eddie knew that much of what he did could have been done by machines. But he was convinced that it should not be.

Eventually, Ovca made her way to Mars, and she and Eddie became a kind of doctor and nurse team. She was married now, and had a child. Her little family took up residence in the expanding warren beneath the monastery.

For a long stretch, Doug had no symptoms of his illness, and he enjoyed his life on Mars. He did not join Eddie in nursing the sick, however. He preferred to stay with the monks and avoid meeting too many new people. He found, again, that he loved farming, and he took charge of a great deal of the growing being done on the abbey's grounds.

The greenhouses were mostly on terraces below the Abbey along the side of the mountain. From a distance, each greenhouse looked about the size of a tool shed, but Olympus Mons is the largest mountain in the solar system, and each tiny-looking greenhouse was actually a self-contained farm.

Doug spent his days in the oldest of the farms, St. Isidore. It was a bright and open green space, divided into nine sections of several acres each. The crops and livestock were rotated through the sections. Three times each day the bells of the St. Isidore Chapel rang the Angelus, and Doug stopped to pray. "The Angel of the Lord declared unto Mary..."

One of the things he liked best about his newfound faith was the peculiar way that Catholics had of marking time. The seasons and the feasts, the praying of the hours, the communal times and the solitary times—he loved the rhythm of it. On the Feast of St. Isidore, for example, a communal Mass was held in the main chapel of the abbey, and then the monks and a large band of lay people processed down to St. Isidore's Farm, where everything—the animals, the plants, the tools, the dirt, and the workers—was blessed by the abbot.

Because Isidore was a Spanish saint, they all then enjoyed a Spanish lunch.

Doug felt that each day was fussed over, and he liked it. He found he had little use for media anymore. He wanted to be with the plants and the animals, or sitting around a dinner table with the monks, or walking with Eddie through the streets of Abbeytown.

"It is harder to get in touch with reality than most people think," he told Eddie on one of their walks. "To really feel the moments of each day, to accept life as the gift it is. To be simple takes a lot of hard work."

"I am glad to have you as a friend, Doug."

After a while, Doug found that he could not walk as long with Eddie anymore, and then it was too much to walk at all. Eddie would push him in a wheelchair sometimes, and the two of them would laugh as much as ever.

He lost things and he gained things. Strangely, he came to see his suffering as one of the gains. He decided that suffering, when it was accepted with love, was a kind of purifying fire. He felt himself growing ready, even eager, for what came next.

"It took me a long time, in the years before I knew you, to accept that I was really and truly a man," Doug told Eddie.

"Those must have been hard years."

"But when you and the bishop came, I learned something even more important," Doug said.

Eddie smiled. "What was it?"

"I learned what a glorious thing it is to be a man."

Doug continued to work on St. Isidore's Farm even when he became quite weak. The doctors had been wrong about one thing; he did not go blind.

He was planting peas at a potting bench when he saw explosions high in the sky above the abbey; a battle was raging in space or at the edge of space.

He felt it coming on, cold and sharp. He felt the tipping and the floor rushing up to smack him on the head. He groaned. He could not move. He was afraid. But he could still see, and through the pea plants he saw the windows of St. Isidore's Chapel, and he heard the bells. "The Angel of the Lord declared unto Mary, and she conceived of the Holy Spirit..." he said quietly.

He smelled the earth, moist and fertile. He was not afraid now.

The battle was below and behind him now. And then no battle was raging anymore.

# EPILOGUE

On this spot was martyred Bishop Mark Gastelum, first native bishop of Mars.

Throughout System War I, and despite constant threats to his life, the bishop resisted the Fascist schismatic churches. He remained the Catholic pastor of Mars even as the planet fell to Fascist forces.

By some accounts, the bishop was personally executed by Fuhrer Joseph Hadamar, though evidence for this is contradictory. What is certain is that Bishop Gastelum, having been cornered with the remains of his flock beside what was then the Cavern Sea, stepped out to greet an armed Fascist contingent with the words, "Love God, my brothers and sisters," and was immediately shot down.

Bishop Gastelum, along with his close confidant, Abbot Edward Cho, is today recognized as co-patron for the Church on Mars. This cathedral was consecrated on the 273rd anniversary of his death.

**Plaque at the foot of the altar,**
**Chasm Cathedral, Coolidge City, Mars**

# ABOUT THE AUTHOR

Cyril Jones-Kellett served for a decade as editor of one of the top Catholic newspapers in the United States—twice leading San Diego's *Southern Cross* to highest honors from the Catholic Press Association of the United States and Canada (CPA). His columns, which have been published in Catholic publications around the country, have won multiple awards, including Best General Interest Column from the CPA.

Before his writing career, he spent time living in an urban Catholic Worker house dedicated to serving homeless men.

Made in the USA
Middletown, DE
17 October 2015